JESSICA WATKINS PRESENTS

BITTER
Root

Y. DEONNA

Songs of Inspiration: Tenth Avenue North-Worn, Yolanda Adams- Open My Heart

Scriptures of Inspiration:
Hebrews 12:15 Look after each other so that none of you fails to receive the grace of God. Watch out that no poisonous root of bitterness grows up to trouble you, corrupting many.

Acts 8:23 For I see that you are in the gall of bitterness and in the bondage of iniquity.

Ephesians 4:31 Let all bitterness and wrath and anger and clamor and slander be put away from you, along with all malice.

<u>Wounded</u>

Now I lay me down to sleep, I pray to God my soul to keep...

I wonder does He even remember me? I said this prayer as a child, followed Him humbly, loved Him with all that was in me, and then I grew up. Wounded by the world, scarred by others words, broken by men who never loved me, chained to the past that is spiritually killing. Will He set me free?

Bound so tightly to the mistakes and held captive by the sins, pleading with God to let me in. The wounds were so deep, attaching to every part of me. Loneliness plagued the deepest parts of my soul. I looked to God, He said come, but I said no, too afraid to surrender. I let go. My heart was shattered by a secret past that refused to be hidden or hushed, haunting me, mocking me, reminding me that I was not good enough. My innocence was stolen, my heart remolded and hardened by the lies men told me, so insecure, so needy for love that I let myself be taken to a godless place. There like trash I was left, burning with pain, bleeding from a betrayal that I didn't see, not until after he wounded me.

Wounded by poisonous, unsaved hands, simple-minded men who only sought to destroy, I fell in sync with their touch. Blistered and branded by the evil that had attached itself to their

4. Deonna

hearts, I was floating further and further from God, too apprehensive to believe the promises written in red, too afraid, thinking I would hear Him deny me too. For my wounds had more power than His word and I believed my sin penetrated too deep, so scripture could not reach. I breathed in Satan's lies like smoke polluting the sky, never reading between the lines, never thinking, or testing to see if it were the truth. I was just too broken, bitter and wounded, to see God was still so very near to me. I just thought no one would love me. I'm no good because too much was stolen too soon. I was no longer me. What can I offer Thee?

If I should die before I wake, I pray to God my soul to take. So young, so naïve, so clueless to the misery, so innocent. Those are days I long for once more. I never questioned, never thought I wasn't good enough, and then it all changed. The injuries came, sometimes so many at one time that I thought I would die, but fear kept me alive. I feared my soul God would not take. It was so corroded and contaminated that I thought He would refuse me. Even I tried to deny me, knowing too well what I allowed to let be, knowing how I leaned on human understanding and self-sufficiency. So foolish I was to think, so young and dumb but even now, somehow I let my past revisit me and it shakes me to my core. I ask myself, "God what am I here for?"

Who will love the woman who has been left behind time after time? The men who said they loved me didn't. My father, who was supposed to set the standard, didn't. How can I, with a wounded soul, a battered and shattered heart, and a bitter root believe that God will love me? I'm good no more. My body is charred by evil men, my heart is detached, my agonies I never could foresee. I'm so lonely.

But didn't God say He would be with me, even to the ends of the Earth? Didn't Christ say that with man these things aren't possible, but with God nothing is impossible? If I'm faithful, won't He be too? He is abundance, and He is the truth.

My wounds have grown and become infected, making me feel so disconnected. I can't deny what I have heard and read, for I can't get God out of my head. He is willing, but I keep pulling away, too afraid of what He will say come Judgment Day.

Confessions I give, not so easy, but if I keep them inside, for sure they will kill me. I don't want to die. I'm guilty of loving the world and of being lukewarm, but please my Father, have mercy on me. In my mind, it was on me to heal the wounds that seemed to always bleed. In my infinite ignorance, I leaped too soon and landed on sinking sand. You warned me, but I didn't understand. This is what came to be. I became a slave to sin and shame and You tried to save me. I want to be saved. I do. I want my wounds to heal as you reveal in the scripture You left behind. I wonder, am I worth being saved? Have I cried one time too many, is there any grace left for me, can I ever be set free? Or, have I given sin the key to come in and out as it pleases, freezing my eternal assets because I feel like a reject?

You see, this is what happens to me. I want to believe. I know the truth. I've read the Bible through and through but I feel like I'm the one whose disobedience went too far, whose sin-scarred skin is already broken and therefore, I fear never to hear these words spoken: "Well done." I wanted so much too soon and jumped ahead of You. Before I understood, I wanted to be like the world. Oh, such a simple minded girl. It was easy for the world to wound me. I was too green to see the danger, too sweet to see manipulation, too kind to see the temptation. Now every second of each day I lay and I wait, conflicted and disturbed by things that didn't have to be; longing like a child who lost a puppy to have my innocence again, to be free of wounds, to no longer be bitter to the root, to be like You. I want to believe the words that I am someone worth dying for, but that seems so foreign for someone like me.

Chapter 1

The honking of a car alarm in the distance woke Sophina up out of a drug-induced sleep. Slowly, her droopy, encrusted, brown eyes opened to a place she wasn't familiar with, but she was growing accustomed to that. There was never any telling where she would wake up. Her life had become a series of cheap motels, endless nights, hard partying and whatever else. It was how she lived. This lifestyle helped keep the past away; a past that had made her bitter and angry. She sighed. She hated thinking, but this was nothing like the life she'd left behind back in North Carolina. A life that seemed to have been ages ago.

The stench of the room finally hit her, a combination of sweat mixed with only God knew what else, violently attacking her senses. She cringed. Instantly, she wanted to be high again and back to sleep. Life was better when she was either asleep or high. Life was better when she was so out of it that she didn't remember her name or what month or season it was. She wondered just how much more abuse her body could take.

Her dry mouth cried for water, but her beaten body was unable to gather the strength to get up. Her chapped lips burned from maltreatment and self-abuse. Not for the first time, she wondered why God allowed her to wake to see another day. It would be like every other day: she'd finally get her body

9. Deonna

working, then shower, sniff, inject and/or smoke whatever concoction that Dante had. Once she had her daily happiness, she would then go work the streets. It was what she needed to do since her sister Semira said she was cutting her off financially, as well as her brother Seth. It wasn't like her baby sister was hurting for money. In fact, neither of them were. Her sister, Semira had a house and was raising Sophina's daughter, so why did she feel the need to cut Soph off? The way Sophina looked at it, her sister owed her. Pushing the past out of her mind, she slowly turned to her left to see if Dante still was in bed, but he wasn't there. She didn't hear the shower running so she assumed he was out hustling or something. Knowing him, he would suggest they pick up and move to another area. He was interested in Nevada and figured that it would be a great place to make money and get lost. It wasn't like she cared much. As long as he kept the candy coming, she wasn't bothered about where they were. She just didn't want to go back to NC and see her judgmental sister. Yeah, there was no way she could go back to NC, not after all the stuff she'd done. Feeling was never good for her, it was why she stayed lit. It was time to be lit again. The emotions and feelings that were being unraveled were not conducive. Nah, she was ready to smoke to oblivion. Hopefully, Dante would be back soon with her "breakfast."

She turned to the other side of the bed, and there, glaring at her like a red flag, was one of those standard Bibles. Seeing it sent shivers down her spine. Her Bible-toting mother had sent her, Semira and Seth to Sunday school and church regularly, no matter the weather. The only time one got out of church was if they had a serious illness or if their father…she didn't finish that thought. Instead, she threw off the dingy comforter and itchy sheets and dragged her drug battered body to the bathroom. She avoided looking in mirrors, too afraid to see the horrible sight she had become. She didn't want to see the truth, not that it mattered, because once she felt like the past was coming back or even her present for that matter, she would just shoot up and feel relief and release. That was what she needed now. The life of a junkie, who had a chemical attachment like herself, only cared about one thing, chasing the next high. Even though a month ago she'd overdosed on heroin and the EMTs had to use norcan (Naloxone) to save her life, her addiction was strong. That should have been enough to make her stop and go to rehab, right, but no, her love her the high was greater than her own life. It was pretty much a given that drugs would kill her, and sometimes she felt what she deserved was a horrible death for what she did to her sister just to get high.

~~~

4. Deonna

"No, get off, Sophina help me, please help me! Please," *Semira screamed.* Her rich sable eyes that felt glued shut flew painfully open. Her breath labored as she sought air, but fear made her inhale too much and she was choking now. Sweat mixed with tears swam down her face, back and arms, saturating her Egyptian cotton sheets which were wrapped around her body like a snake. She looked around, but no one was there, only darkness. She still shook with fear, shame, and anger. It was just another nightmare from a past she thought she'd buried deep. Shaking her head in dismay, she grabbed the face towel off of the nightstand to clean herself up.

"Be calm, just take slow deep breaths," she told herself. She was stronger than this. As much as she'd survived in her childhood and adulthood, she could overcome this setback as well. Tonight, she'd probably slipped because of being overly stressed out.

As the fear eased and calm slowly encased her, she inhaled and exhaled slowly all while reciting the Lord's Prayer. It helped to soothe her. Once she collected herself, she got up and walked softly across the carpeted floor and out of her bedroom to check on Nalani, who was sound asleep. Her sweet French vanilla mocha blend face held a peaceful smile and an innocent glow. She was holding her Tigger tightly to her chest. For her, the world was perfect. Semira touched Nalani's skin gently, just like her mother used to do her, pulled her covers up, and kissed Nalani tenderly. At least, her cries and screams didn't stir her little one from her gentle slumber.

Feeling relieved that Nalani was comforted, Semira walked downstairs and began checking all the locks on the doors, windows, and making sure the alarm system was on. She was always so paranoid after having a nightmare. Now she needed to be comforted. This was a process she did at least twice a night. Finally, she felt stable and safe, at least for now. With the assurance that the house was secure, she walked into the custom made kitchen she had remodeled last year, seeking the refrigerator. A smile spread across her bright face as she reached out for the chocolate milk and poured it into the tea mug Nalani made her in Girl Scouts, and then placed it into the microwave to warm it. For her, warm chocolate milk always helped her sleep better. She blew in the teacup to cool her milk, sipped it, and felt the way it dressed her insides and coated her stomach. She closed her eyes and let the feeling overtake her.

It was annoying that at her age she still had nightmares. She was so angry with herself for allowing the fear to enter back into her heart. She'd kicked it out years ago and promised herself never to let it back in, never to think of it, and never to speak of the shame, the ungodly sins, the bitterness, the secrets and unseen wounds. So long she thought she was in control of the past, but it seemed that her past was controlling her. Usually, her nightmares occurred when she was stressed and worried about something, mostly her older sister, Sophina or Soph as they called her, but she hadn't been that person in a long time.

The warm milk chocolate coated her pain, a temporary antidote for the perfidy, ignorance and greed of her older sister. Sophina was the catalyst of the hurt, the bitterness and the problems that Semira now faced. It seemed like that was all Sophina wanted out of life; to hurt others as much as she possibly could. Her sister, how she loved and loathed her. They had once been close sisters and best friends. Semira idolized Sophina until her sister betrayed her, not once, but twice. No one knew the truth because Semira had kept silent. She was always in Sophina's shadow, never as pretty, never as lovely, never as popular and never as fun because she chose to be responsible. Whereas, Sophina was irresponsible. Sadly, that made her sister unable to face the ramifications of her actions and mistakes. Shaking her head at that truth, Semira was flooded with memories of the past and her heart hurt.

What horror they'd suffered at the hands of their mother's ex-husband and then the personal horror she'd survived after her sister's betrayal. The family knew the temperament of Samson, their father. Semira was the baby of the family, and was also the one who got abused the most. She couldn't fight back. Even when she had been the one doing right, she was somehow wrong. However, her sister, no matter what she did, was quickly forgiven. Even Samson seemed to be gentler with her sister. Her family seemed to always find an excuse for Sophina's behavior. Semira believed with all her being that that treatment led her sister down a wayward path that was slowly killing her. For her sister, life was a party.

While Sophina partied and got asked on dates, Semira read books and studied. But there were times, very brief moments, when she wanted to be like Sophina before she changed. Times before she chose the world and not the Word. Unlike Sophina, Semira didn't like getting into trouble, and she didn't like feeling the backhand of Samson's hand. Semira wanted to be good, and Sophina loved being bad. Then it all changed. What and why was beyond her understanding. She couldn't, even after several years, understand what she'd done to offend Sophina so deeply.

Semira let out a sigh. This was not what God wanted her to do. It was dangerous to linger even for a second in the past because it awakened things that should forever stay dormant, reopening wounds that had never fully healed. When a person awakened past issues before their time, it unleashed a concoction of bitterness, hate, sin, and revenge, which was a

4. Deonna

horrible path to a place she tried to forget the direction of. The sound of her neighbor's dog barking startled her thoughts. She took that as a warning from God, telling her to come back to the present and stay away from the past that sometimes felt like the present. Rubbing the side of her temple, she slowly walked upstairs into her bedroom and rested her swirling head on the pillow. Sleep was not ready to yield to her, so she picked up her Bible and read 1 John, seeking solace and refuge in her time of desperate need.

"Father, you know the sins, the pain, the unspeakable that has occurred, take it from me. Father, please heal the hurt. Help me to love not hate, forgive and not seek revenge. In Jesus' sweet name, Amen," she whispered and drifted back to sleep. She needed to settle her soul, find a way to heal her wounds. The paranoia and fear needed to disappear forever because if not, it would corrode any good thing and all of her blessings. She had to let go. Lord knows, she had lost enough already. There wasn't much else left.

~~~

The morning brought relaxation and a new perspective as Semira finished doing her quiet time and meditated on verse 1 Peter 4:8 NKJV *"and above all things have fervent love for one another, for love will cover a multitude of sins."* That helped her put her things back into focus so that she could get

12

her mind on her job. She pulled into her parking space ready for a day of challenging work. Though it was winter, the sun still shone brightly, kissing the fresh salted pavement, and the rays' shine warmed her cold body. She told herself today would be a good day. "This is the day that the Lord has made, I will rejoice and be glad in it," she recited inwardly. She again reburied the nightmare that had found its way into her bedroom. She didn't want to recall it or analyze it any longer. What was done, was done.

Semira let out a sigh of confidence and walked into readying work. This was her place. She had worked in the bank since she was sixteen-years-old. She loved it! She enjoyed the people, her co-workers, and her bosses. Here, no one cared about her past because it didn't matter. All that mattered was that she got the job done and did it well. The bank had been voted number one in customer satisfaction again for the fifth year in a row. It was because of Semira's new policies, how she interacted with the community, and her dedication to using the Servant Leadership model when interacting with her staff. It worked wonders and everyone truly cared about each other.

Entering into the bank, she had a pleasant surprise waiting for her. Thomas Calloway. He was the owner of the local NFL team and one of her most loyal and faithful clients. He was also very dear to her because they shared a secret. He had been her support at a time when she'd felt she had none. Since that time, he'd always been there for her. Mr. Calloway was the father she wished she had, although her stepfather was an exceptional man as well. However, there was something special about Mr. Calloway. He was a young, fifty-five-year-old that stood about six-feet tall and every bit a silver fox. He wore his age very well as he invested a great deal of time in taking care of his body. He was fit, handsome, polite and sincerely kind, and even though he was very wealthy, he was a godly man. Money was not his love, but God was. That made him different from most billionaires. He knew the difference between a self-made man and a Christ made man.

Today, he wore his signature Kiton K-50 suit and a silk blue tie that matched his youthful eyes. Semira smiled when she noticed he was wearing the custom made football sapphire encrusted cufflinks she gifted him last Christmas. It was an expensive gift that he more than deserved. He really was an awesome guy. There was this gentle air about him. He was calming and fatherly. He had three sons, was a pillar of the community, and good to Forrester and Rhodes, the bank that Semira managed.

Over the years, the bank had grown into an international financial and management institution to the wealthiest people around. Semira was part of the reason why they had Mr.

Calloway's business and the rest of the athletes because she knew how to make money and build relationships. She interacted well with any person when it dealt with business, which was surprising considering her background. She was never one for self-pity. She believed in making changes, not complaining. In her early twenties, she graduated college with a dual degree in Business Administration and Accounting. Recently, she graduated from graduate school with a dual Masters in Business Administration and Trust and Wealth Management from Campbell University in Buies Creek, and she was a certified public accountant, all achieved by the age of twenty-five. She liked being an overachiever. It was her way of burying the past and cleaning up what was filthy in her mind. Pulling herself back to present, Semira knew Mr. Calloway had not scheduled an appointment to see her, so she gathered this was a social call.

"Hey, Mr. Calloway, and to what do I owe the pleasure?" she queried as she opened her office door and stood aside so he could enter first. She had rearranged the office a week earlier because she wanted something more updated, modern, and polished for the clientele she interacted with. Her best friend and sister girl, Mariah came in and redesigned it. Semira thought it was very nice and professional looking. She could tell by Mr. Calloway's face that he liked it as well.

4. Deonna

"You make me feel old when you call me mister, Semira. Just call me Tom or Dad, like everybody else. You are the daughter I always wanted," he gushed, sitting down in the plush leather chair, his gaze never breaking as if he was attempting to read the thoughts in her mind.

She walked around her desk and sat down looking at him with smiling eyes. "Sorry, I just can't call my friends' dad by his first name or dad. I don't think it is professional," she replied, smiling back at him. He was always pleasant like that. He did act like a dad to her. What they shared, her father nor her stepfather knew, not even her mother. Just Mr. Calloway. He respectfully kept her secret to himself. She was eternally grateful.

"I know you're always the professional. You act like my eldest son," he teased with a chuckle. She was so much like him that it was scary. "I came here to invite you to a party I'm having at the house. You have not come to any functions lately. I know you are busy, but Langston Forrester is going to have to allow you time off so that you can have a social life." He grinned. He knew how hard she worked and how her childhood was stolen and it pained him. "Besides, look at it as a chance to get more business for the bank. You are great at finance, banking, consulting and managing. A lot of my associates need someone like you. Will you come?" he asked, already making up in his mind that he would not take no for an answer. He wanted her to be more social. A young beautiful woman like her needed to be out and about. He worried she worked too hard and busied herself too much to avoid the past trauma of her childhood, a childhood he wished he could have altered. Her sister and brother suffered harshly at the hands of a man he once held a great deal of respect for. He never knew Samson, the man who had been his maintenance supervisor, had beat his family and ruled with an iron fist.

She thought for a moment. She was not the party type, and any off time she had she liked to spend with family and friends. She knew some people liked to mix business and pleasure, but not her. In her mind, work was work and personal was personal. At the same time, she was the head of the bank and wanted to maintain appearances. Maybe she should go because this was really a great opportunity. "I can do that. Let me know the time, place and what to wear. If you don't mind, I'd like to bring my best friend. She'd really enjoy meeting some of the company that you will have," she replied.

He lifted his hands as if he was praising God. "Awesome! You can invite who you like just as long as you come. I have your invitation right here. I hope to see you tomorrow night," he giddily replied with a big smile and walked over to kiss her cheek. She had the most radiant face, as lovely as her mother's. She made him so proud. He knew her past and her pain well, and still she'd triumphed over adversity like it was nothing more than a puddle. She was an inspiration to him. So many times he wanted to reveal so much to her, but he stayed silent. No time ever seemed to be a good time and she was in a good place.

He waved goodbye and walked down the stairs glowing with excitement that she agreed to come. The next step would be prying her away from the bank to run his financial empire.

Once Semira was sure he was out of hearing, she let out a yelp of excitement and danced around her office. This was big! Mr. Calloway was the man. He had wealth and then his first wife's family had money as well. She passed away from breast cancer after years of battling the disease, but he bounced back with a younger, international brunette. He never missed a beat. Semira was not sure if she was with him because she loved him or what he could provide her, and she guessed he was not sure either because he got a prenuptial agreement. She and his oldest son had gone over it with a fine-toothed comb.

Semira and Thomas' son, Blaine, had graduated high school together and attended the same college. That was how Mr. Calloway and she became close. Well, actually it was her senior year in high school when she won an award for the business proposal she did for FBLA (Future Business Leaders of America). Mr. Calloway was just always there. Blaine was into sports, but he liked owning the team better than playing for the team. His younger brother, Camden, played baseball and was very good, being signed to a major league team. The oldest, Thomas Jr., was the snobbiest, handsome but snobby. He was not at all athletic, but he was business and legal-minded. He found the perfect girl who was equally annoying and nicknamed herself the Duchess. The entire family adored Semira and she, them. She was the only one who was allowed to call Thomas Jr., TJ. For the most part, they all had a good heart like their father. Two out of his three sons inherited his love for community and those who lived in it. He made sure his players were the same. His eldest son, not so much. Semira assumed there was one in every family. God knows her sister Sophina was it for their family.

She settled into work and phoned Mariah to tell her about the invitation, and just as she thought, Mariah was ready to party. After Semira left work, she went to pick up Nalani, took her to her grandmother's house, and drove into the city to meet Mariah so that they could find appropriate outfits.

Shopping was not as enjoyable for Semira as it was for Mariah. She was madam fashionista and Semira was more, well not so "fashion-gifted." She wanted anything that would cover her from head to toe. Mariah wanted anything that would

Y. Deonna

showcase her from head to toe. Semira watched with amazement as Mariah navigated through the variety of clothing and found dress after dress for Semira as well as for her. Unlike Mariah, Semira didn't like being the center of attention when it came to men. If it didn't have anything to do with business, then she preferred not to be engaged with the male gender. Keeping that rule made life less complicated and a little lonely at times, but less complicated.

Chapter 2

Sophina sat huddled in a corner surrounded by her own vomit and blood. This particular man she had been with was too violent and he didn't pay. Instead, he beat her and she was too scared to move. She heard him shuffling around the motel room and she wished he would leave. She didn't know where Dante was. He never left her alone this long before and she was scared that she might die. She leaned her head back, and closed her eyes. Instantly, she was back in time. She fought as hard as she could to wake up. Sleeping was horrible torture and she didn't want to remember those times.

"Soph, wake up! Get up, we've got to go," Dante told her. He'd beaten the man who had hurt her and robbed him, and they needed to get on the road before the dude woke up.

"I can't, Dante. I hurt, all over."

"I know. Come on, we got to go before the law arrives."

She attempted to nod, but it was too difficult so she allowed him to help her. The last thing she saw while he carried her battered body was the standard Bible and just like always, it mocked her. She felt such bitterness when she saw it because it reminded her of what her sister was and what she would never be.

~~~

4. Deonna

Walking into the mansion was like walking into another country. Semira had been at the Calloway estate before, but it seemed more elegant than she last remembered. Marble countertops, wooden floors, Italian ceilings painted by hand. It was what she thought billionaires lived in. It seemed the newest Mrs. Calloway had expensive taste. Semira stood in awe momentarily. Mariah grabbed her hand and led her into the main room. There were crowds of people walking in and out. Semira just smiled and nodded, trying to be as sociable as she could.

"Semira, there you go." Blaine grinned, walking up to her, hugging her and then hugging Mariah. "You ladies look so lovely, come on so I can show you off," he complimented, offering each of them his arm. They talked about their old college days. Those days were so far and foreign to Semira. Days that held secrets and heartbreaks and just the thought of it made her recall Natano, another part of her past she wanted to forever bury. She had been so in love with him, and she thought he'd loved her too, but things happened. Things seemed to always happen and that was why she shut down her heart. It could not get broken if she didn't share it.

Her friends noticed that she was taking a vacation from the conversation, so they reeled her back in by Blaine asking her about Sophina. He had not seen her in a while and was wondering if she was okay.

Hearing him mention her sister's name sent a shock wave through Semira's body. She had not heard from her in a while and tonight was not the night she wanted to talk about her. She said very little and changed the subject quickly. Mariah felt her feelings and took Blaine away, leaving Semira alone. She let out a sigh of relief. She attempted to smile and greet prospective clients, but the truth was, this was not her scene. She was not on top of her game. She didn't like big crowds or lusting and leering eyes. She didn't care to hear how beautiful she was or strangers placing their unwanted hands on her shoulder or small of her back. It felt like a violation.

She saw Thomas Calloway and he came to greet her. It was like he could read her thoughts and knew how uncomfortable she was. A part of her hated that feeling, but she was thankful for Mr. Calloway being very attentive and asking if she were in need of anything. Semira told him she was fine and to entertain his guest. She saw Mariah flirting and having a good time, so she found a quiet place to sit. She sat there observing, thinking, and praying that the time would pass quickly and no one would bother her.

Her mind kept contemplating her past, her sister and her sister's many secrets. For some reason, it was bothering her more than it used to. She had a few of her own and now, it seemed like they wanted to be told. She was not ready. *Would she ever be?* She felt confessing them made them real, but if she kept them secret, she could deny that anything bad had ever happened, at least for a while. It would be nice for just a moment to be free of secrets and fears. She wished she was like Mariah and more of a conversationalist, carefree and able to interact with any type of social situation, but she wasn't. Men made her nervous, especially if the conversation had to do with anything other than business. Sometimes she felt like she had this neon sign that suggested she was a target. It was why she overcompensated so much. That too was a secret.

"Hey, Semira, how are you doing?" Thomas Jr. questioned as he walked toward her. He'd notice how she shied away from the groups and found a place of solitude.

A smile creased her lips. "Hey, TJ, how are you?" she countered. She was the only person who referred to him as such, and when one of his college pals attempted to do the same, TJ quickly put him in his place. He looked like a pretty rich boy, but he had some hands on him too.

"I'm great. It is good to see you. I don't get to see you much, as I'm often out of town or the country," he stated.

She nodded. That was true. He was always somewhere with his lady friend. "I know you are super busy. How is, um, what's her name, Bessie?" Semira queried.

"Oh no, it's Benita. She's in France. I'm flying out tomorrow to be with her," he replied as he sat down beside Semira. "You know, I really hate these functions. I so hate dealing with all these fake people."

Semira smiled but didn't reply. She hated these events too, but it was part of her occupation to interact and attract new business to the bank. Besides, this was a Calloway function and that was big business.

He took that as her agreeing with him and continued talking. "Well, at least, you are here. I have someone on my level to converse with," he added.

"I'm not much for the conversation today. I'm a bit tired," Semira confessed. It was true, this entire process drained her.

"Well then, we'll just sit here silently together. I refuse to walk among those people anymore. If you feel sleepy, you can rest yourself on my shoulder," he offered kindly.

Semira was surprised by his soft tone and gentleness. However, instead of resting her head on him, she just leaned on him. An hour or two later, Mariah was ready to leave, and they prepared to leave the mansion, but made sure to say their goodbyes to the host.

As they got into the car, Mariah talked nonstop about the football players she met and the businessmen she had been introduced to. Semira tuned in and out, not because she didn't want to hear what she had to say, but because her mind was traveling back in time. It was like a disease. Her mind just time traveled whenever it wanted to without permission. She just was not ready to relive that time. It was a secret for a reason. Her hands began to shake as she tried to pull herself away from trespassing upon the past again. Mariah was still talking and driving and didn't notice anything. Semira rolled down the window hoping that the winter breeze would hush and ease her uncontrollable thoughts. It was imprisoning at times, to be confined to those horrible thoughts.

"Se Se, are you sick? Please roll up the window because it is wintertime," Mariah whined, glancing at her friend like she had lost her mind.

"I'm sorry. I just needed some air," Semira replied, feeling a little better.

Mariah's facial expression turned to concern. "What's the matter anyway? We were in a billionaire's house who invited the who's who of Carolina society and you were hiding out. There were single, available, intelligent men and you were hiding." Mariah fussed. She could not understand why someone would do that. Semira was young, beautiful and talented. How she flaked at the biggest social gathering of the year was beyond Mariah's comprehension. Men were checking for her and she was ducking them.

"You should have a cell phone full of numbers. I do," she bragged with a flirty smile.

Semira rolled her eyes in her head. "I'm good. Besides, I made several contacts and handed out all of my business cards." In her mind, that was a success. She hadn't come to the party to find her soul mate. It was not even time for that. She had more important matters to deal with.

"There is more to life than working all the time. You are allowed to have fun, interact with people and date a little. How is Nalani going to learn about men if you don't bring any into her life?" she queried.

What did she know about raising kids? Semira had a father and he'd taught her nothing. She loved her stepfather, but she could have done without Samson. She thought she came out of it well. It wasn't that she was a man hater, she was just cautious. Her daughter had a great uncle.

"She has a wonderful uncle who gives her all the attention she needs. He's a great male role model, as well as Blaine, TJ, and Cam." Sometimes Mariah was just as bad as

4. Deonna

Semira's mom. Unlike either of them, Semira didn't have to have a man. She knew who she was. Her identity was not going to be made better or lessen because of the addition or subtraction of a man. She liked herself and she was teaching Nalani to be independent of man and Christ-sufficient. Besides, she trusted herself. She knew too well what happened to women who fell for the lustful lyrics that men spoke. They ended up battered, broken and bitter. That was not her and she was going to set a better example for Nalani. She deserved that.

"So you are just going to tune me out?" Mariah fussed.

"No. You're my best friend and I appreciate your concern. I'm not ready to date," she confessed. That was the honest to God truth. Semira let out a sigh of relief as Mariah pulled into Semira's driveway. She wanted the conversation ended.

Mariah, on the other hand, wished her friend would stop pretending like she didn't want more of a social life or a man. It was time for her to move on, forget about everything, and start anew. It was apparent that Semira wasn't her sister, and every man wasn't Samson. All men didn't abuse their wives and children. Semira was her own person, yet it seemed the actions and pain she suffered from her childhood still haunted her now. "All right, girl. I love you. I'll call you when I get home,"

Mariah promised. Though she wanted to say more, she knew it wasn't the time.

Semira smiled and offered her a hug before exiting the car. Then she quickly ran into the house, rested her body on the couch, and closed her eyes. Instantly, her thoughts went to her sister. Even though Sophina wasn't there, she was still weighing heavily on Semira's mind. She feared so badly what Sophina was doing, and whom she was doing it with. Sophina needed to come back home and let the family help her. She needed to face her demons and take care of the mess she left behind. The entire family was paying for her sins. God knew Semira and Nalani had paid the highest cost.

Y. Deonna

Chapter 3

"Burr…" Semira hummed to herself as the winter air rushed against her apricot skin. She was glad that she had put on some extra lotion, or she would be as white as the Snowman she and Nalani had created yesterday. She winced as the cold air seeped through her scarf, but it was a beautiful snowy Carolina day. The snow covered ground looked like a blanket from heaven, and Semira smiled at how lovely God made everything. She took a deep breath, closed her eyes for a moment, and thought to herself how much she loved winter. A day perfect for skiing or sledding, just the thought made her body shiver with excitement. Maybe later she and Nalani could do some winter activities. She believed in keeping Nalani busy, that way she would not end up like Sophina.

Semira pulled her coat tighter, grabbed Nalani's hand and they made a mad dash to the car, crushing the snow below.

"I beat you, Auntie. I got here first, *haha*!!" her little voice echoed.

Semira had to laugh at her. Nalani was missing her two front teeth. Semira couldn't believe how she was growing up because it seemed just like yesterday she was teething. It looked like Nalani was going to be tall like Seth and Semira. Sophina took after their momma and was short at five and a half feet— just petite little ladies. Seth and Semira took after their biological father's side of the family. They were all tall and slender. Of course, Semira was curvier than her slender relatives, but it worked.

"Yeah, Nalani, you beat Auntie this time. Come on, let me see that pretty smile. We are about to visit G-momma." Nalani's face brightened up, and she began to do the wiggle. They both loved going to momma's house for dinner because she made the best southern food in all North Carolina. Just the thought of it made Semira's toes curl up.

She buckled Nalani in and they were off. Nalani liked to sing to her Veggie Tales disc, so Semira hummed along with her. Her curls bounced along as she drove the twenty-minute ride to her momma's house.

"Okay, Nalani, it's time to get out," Semira told her niece as she turned the engine off.

"Okay, Auntie, I bet I will beat you again." She took off like a bullet and Semira knew she could never catch up. Nalani ran right to her G-Momma. Semira loved to see her happy. She was so much better now; no one could tell by looking that she was a premature baby. Semira walked in the house behind her and the smell of deep fried catfish, cabbage, cornbread, and fried corn came at once, making Semira's stomach growl. "Momma, that food sure does smell good."

4. Deonna

A warm smile grew on her mother's face. "Well thank you, baby, you know I try." She sent Nalani to the kitchen and gave her daughter a hug. "How are you doing, Semira?" Her eyes squinted as if she was trying to read her before she could speak. Semira knew that look of hers, she had seen it many times before. The talk was coming. She wished her stepdaddy had been home because if he was, he would guide the conversation away from her lack of dating and being single.

"I'm fine, Momma. Nalani is fine. My sister, on the other hand, well I have no idea. The last I heard she had followed that man to Las Vegas, California or Miami; some fast-paced place like that. You know, Nalani does not even ask me about her anymore," Semira intoned as she took off her coat and shoes. She loved to feel the soft carpet kiss her feet. "In fact, Sophina doesn't even call anymore. I've been thinking it's time to adopt Nalani. I haven't told her, but what do you think? I have had her since she was born so I might as well," Semira queried as she leaned back and rested her long legs on the sofa.

Ella gave her that motherly look and Semira did her best not to show the frustration she was feeling. Their mother always held out for Sophina, but she never got better, and she never cared what she was doing to Nalani. She only cared for herself, but her mother believed that Sophina was the prodigal son and would come home clean, saved and renewed. Semira knew the truth. She knew how sadistic her sister could be, especially when she was under the influence. Unlike her mother naively believed, her oldest daughter was not always the victim. Most of the time, Semira felt like her sister was the villain, but those were only thoughts she shared with her journal. She would never say it to anyone else. The unnecessary pain Sophina inflicted upon her was self-served, and sometimes that made Semira want to hurt her just as bad. However, she knew that was not the way to be. Even though Sophina was methodical, mental and manipulative like their biological father, none of that was even part of Semira's or her brother, Seth's DNA. It often confounded her how they could be so different and all come from the same people. The thought of what her sister had allowed to happen, and what she was probably doing made her body shiver. Semira knew too well what her older sister was capable of: anything.

Ella shook her head. She knew if they were patient and kept praying, Sophina would come back to them. "Well, baby, I don't know if you should do that. I mean, when Sophina comes back, you know she might want to take on that motherly role again. I think things are fine the way they are. What more you want?" she questioned, not understanding why at this age the two of them still had sibling rivalry. It always hurt her to know her daughters were at odds, but it hurt worse that neither told

4. Deonna

her about Nalani until way after Sophina gave birth. It was easy for them to hide, and she expected that from Sophina, but never Semira.

Semira shook her head in disbelief. Sometimes, she felt like her mother was mad that she got Nalani and she didn't. Ella always took Sophina's side, even when Sophina was the aggressor.

"I don't want anything, Momma." It didn't matter what she said. Semira knew what was best for Nalani. That was the main reason she began to talk to an attorney. It was time to give Nalani a real family. If Sophina ever got Nalani back, she would destroy her. Her sister was the human form of the devil. All she knew how to do was lie, destroy, hurt and then blame her failures on everyone except herself. She was great at displacing the responsibility.

Semira got off the couch, walked to the kitchen, and fixed herself as well as Nalani, a plate. Nalani had long disappeared upstairs to play with her cousin, Tobias, her older and only brother's son. "Momma, where is Seth?" Semira asked, noticing neither he nor Beth were around. It kind of seemed strange because Seth and Tobias were joined at the hip like she and Nalani. Semira guessed that came from their childhood.

"You know, he had to work today and so did Beth. Some emergency at the hospital. So Seth brought Tobias over here. I love having my house filled with my grandbabies. It just makes my life," she crooned with a faraway look in her eye.

"Oh, Momma, you act like you're some old lady. You are just fifty and you look forty so stop acting like that. I'm going to tell Daddy," Semira teased with a hint of laughter. Her mother smiled back at her and patted her back.

"Tobias and Nalani, get your little butts down here, your Auntie Semira has fixed y'all plates, so come and get it," Ella yelled through the house.

Semira heard their little feet pounding the floor, and in a blink of an eye, there were two smiling faces looking at her. "All right you two, which one of you is going to say grace?" They both raised their hands, so Semira told them both to say the grace. Ella had outdone herself, and she had even made peach pie and homemade ice cream. Semira had a great time and so did Nalani.

"Auntie Semira, do you think I can spend the night with G-Momma and Tobias?" Nalani inquired, giving her Auntie her biggest and brightest smile. The smile that got her anything she wanted.

"Sweetie, we had a date for Saturday, remember?" Semira reminded her. She liked spending her weekends with

4. Deonna

Nalani, teaching her educational things and playing games with her. At no time did she want her to look back on her childhood and feel like she didn't have everything she needed. It was important for Semira to do all the things for Nalani that no one had done for her. Her mother worked all the time as a nurse, and Samson was just a bully when he wasn't working. A mean old drunk with a hard right hook and mean left uppercut from his glorious boxing days. She disliked him. After he lost his job at the stadium, he seemed to get worse. Thank God her momma remarried a better man, but the damage was already done. That was damage that Semira wanted to save Nalani and Tobias from. The kind of damage that changed a good person to a bitter one.

"I know, Auntie, but Tobias is staying the whole weekend and I want to stay too. I have some clothes and you can bring me more tomorrow. Please, oh please!" Then she bumped Tobias so he could beg her too.

How could she say no to those two cuties? "Okay, but only if Momma says it is all right." Semira looked at her mom and she nodded in agreement. Ella loved having the children stay with her. Semira thought that after she had gotten her out of the house, she wouldn't want any more children, but she loved being a grandmother. "Well then, it is settled. You are staying with your grandmother for the weekend. However, if you start missing me you just call and I will come get you." Semira was kind of sad to leave Nalani behind.

After dinner, Semira washed the dishes, cleaned the kitchen, and then she sat down and talked to her momma for a while. Her mind wondered what she would do since Nalani had plans. There was something to do. She just had to find it.

"So, baby, what are you going to do with your weekend off?" Ella asked with a smile. She was hoping her daughter would go out, have fun, and do the things young people her age should do.

Semira looked at her and poked out her lip. "I don't know, Momma. I really wanted to spend the day with Nalani, but she wants to be with Tobias. I don't know what to do. I guess I can sleep late, eat fatty foods, and watch all my Tyler Perry movies," she lamented and then smiled to show she was only joking. She'd have an at home spa day and just take a break. That was something she hadn't ever done. She never stopped. Her life was God, Nalani, work, then family and friends. There was always something that needed her attention. She was always busy.

Ella cleared her throat and looked at Semira. "You know, you should go out with that nice young man at church. You know, Moses' son."

4. Deonna

Momma and her matchmaking skills. Semira was somewhat afraid of them seeing that she and Samson had been an imperfect match. Honestly, Semira didn't need her mother's assistance in the male department. She was fine on her own. She had her reasons for remaining single. It wasn't from lack of interest from men, it was her lack of confidence in them. "Momma, I don't have time to date and you know I have to be careful with Nalani. Things are different now."

Her mother sucked her teeth. "You're making excuses. You need a man. You should be dating. You are almost twenty-five years old and you should be having fun. Instead, you act like you are some old lady. Now, I admire you for raising your sister's child, but I think you are neglecting yourself. It is okay to date and to allow a man in your space," Ella fussed, putting her hands on her hips.

Semira rolled her eyes and shook my head. *Need a man?* Maybe her mother felt it necessary to have a man, but she felt it necessary only to have God. Men were problems. They cheated, lied, mistreated and failed. She worked too hard to fall back now. As far as she could see, there was nothing a man had that she wanted. "Momma, I'm not looking for a relationship. I like Nalani's and my life as it is. We don't need a man."

Ella looked at her daughter sideways. She always knew that Semira was a special kind of different, but everyone needed a helpmate. Her daughter was so wrapped up in proving she could do it all that she failed to see the importance of having another there. In this situation, Ella blamed herself because she'd set a bad example that seemed to have damaged her daughter far deeper than she ever thought. It was time to correct that. "You do need a helpmate to have a relationship with, someone to talk to and enjoy. God gave Adam a helpmate for a reason, and God would give you one too if you stopped being so hateful. It's past time. How many times must I tell you this? You're a great catch! Besides, I want more grandbabies," she concluded, not understanding why someone like her wasn't knocking the men off with a broomstick. It was time for her to let go of the past and start allowing herself happiness.

Semira hated when she did this. It was not like she didn't know who she was. She didn't need her mother to remind her, not about her lack of a social life or how great a catch she was. None of that mattered. Men didn't care. They were greedy. Men didn't want worthy women; they preferred slut buckets. All she wanted to do was eat and be merry with her family, not have her mother pester her about dating.

"Momma, I'm going home. Tell Nalani to call me before she goes to sleep. I love you." She kissed her cheek and walked to her car. She loved her momma, but she was a busybody and she knew everything…or so she thought. Today

4. Deonna

just wasn't the day to start that drama. She didn't like her mother telling her she needed to get a man. However, she would never say anything disrespectful to her.

A relaxed calm eased through Semira's body as she arrived home. Once inside, she decided to clean the house. Cleaning was therapeutic for her. The smell of a cleaned house gave her a sense of accomplishment. Just as she started mopping the kitchen floor, her phone began to ring. She ran to pick it up. "Hello?"

"Hey, Semira, it's your best friend, Mariah. So what are you doing tonight?" she asked, hoping they would not be watching Netflix, eating ice cream and chocolate clusters, or worse, watching the Veggie Tale movie marathon with Nalani. Ever since Nalani was born, Semira was becoming more introverted and less social. It was like pulling teeth to get her to go out. She was boring and had been since after freshman year of college. She was old before her time.

"Nothing. Nalani is spending the night with my momma, so I'm cleaning up the house." She could hear Mariah's eyes rolling because she swore that Semira was a neat freak. She and her siblings were raised that cleanliness was next to godliness. It was ingrained into their psyche like it was the eleventh commandment. Though she'd never read it in the Bible, not in

Hebrew, Greek, or English, Samson had sworn it was in there. It wasn't.

"What? You are cleaning the house on a Friday night? Have you lost your mind?" Semira must have changed the schedule because she thought it was Tuesday, Thursday, and Saturday.

Semira could hear the drama in her voice. That was Mariah, always so dramatic.

"I haven't lost my mind, but you know since I have Nalani, I really have gotten into this routine that I like." It was not the greatest, but it worked for her. Semira put on her pajamas and rollers by eight o'clock p.m., then fixed either a cup of lavender tea to sleep or warm chocolate milk. She liked it that way. She didn't want her mind to linger because when it did, she always ended up in tears. She just wanted to be over all the hurt and pain. If she stayed on schedule, then she didn't have time to trespass into the past. Sometimes, it still found her. A word, a sound, or a smell would trigger a flashback into memory, and she was back in that place, where she was helpless and trapped. At one time, she thought she might have a mild case of PTSD, but she wasn't sure if that were true for her because that only happened to soldiers; people who'd had true traumatic events. For some reason, she felt like her attack wasn't that severe. She just needed to get over herself and push forward. At some point, her past would no longer hold her hostage. She'd sworn to herself to never be helpless again. It was why she graduated college and graduate school so quickly. She never wanted to depend on anyone for anything. Her motto was simple, "People let you down, but God pulls you up." She made sure to stay in God.

"Oh my goodness, you are such an old lady. Girl, go put on some nice clothes, well something sexy, we are going to the club, not the church. It is celebrity Friday and ladies get in free, and we are VIP. I need you to take a shower and I'm coming over because you need some guidance," Mariah ordered. Semira was just an old lady, and it was embarrassing. She was still young and needed an active social life. Instead, she hid behind her profession and Nalani.

Why couldn't they go to a church function? A movie or maybe out for something to eat? A club was for young women with no family and no cares. Clubs were crowded, girls got drugs slipped into their drinks, and usually bullets went flying and fights broke out. Why would she want to go to a club? Besides, her attire was all business, business casual, and church clothes. She wasn't sexy, nor did she want to be. She let out a grunt and hung up the phone to take a shower.

Semira had not seen the inside of a club since before Nalani was born, so she turned on the television to music videos. She needed to learn some dance moves to make sure she still had the groove. She knew Mariah would be surprised if she couldn't keep up with her, or maybe she would expect it. There was a time in high school, before her sister became a drug-deranged junkie, when they would all go out and dance until their feet hurt. There was a time when Sophina was fun, when she still cared, until she met bad boys and drugs allowing both to ruin the woman she used to be. Semira didn't know how to help her anymore and she wasn't sure if she really wanted to. In fact, if she was honest, she liked that Sophina was gone. There was peace.

She shook the thought and lotioned down her body. If she didn't have the dance moves, she sure would smell good. As she slipped on her robe, she heard the doorbell ringing. Semira dashed into the front room to let Mariah in. "Hey, sister girl, you look wonderful as always," Semira complimented as she leaned in to hug her friend. Mariah was sparkling. She looked beautiful in her yellow ensemble. Mariah had a rocking body that all men loved. She was thick in all the right places and slender in others. She had this essence about herself that allowed her to command an entire room. She was a universal beauty.

"Okay, girl, I have brought several of my outfits, and we will see what looks good on you." She pushed Semira into the

4. Deonna

bathroom and made her try on every single outfit. Semira liked them all. She hadn't dressed up in a long time and she liked feeling pretty. "Mariah, I like the fabric of this one, but you can see through it. That is so un-lady like, plus it is cold," she complained. Mariahknew she was a Christian woman and she was all about being modest. The outfit was far from being modest.

"Semira, it isn't. We won't be standing in the line, and that outfit will make men lose their breaths. I'm telling you, your body looks good. Have you been going to the gym without me? You know we are supposed to be like Oprah and Gayle, you go and I go and vice versa?" She started staring at her as if she might lie, even going so far as to cock her head sideways and then suck her teeth.

"I only go when you go. I just haven't been eating like I should. I'm just worried, about Sophina, about Nalani, about my family in general. I just don't want any surprises," Semira confessed. She knew she was a walking contradiction when it came to Sophina, but it was her sister.

Mariah huffed and rolled her eyes. "Semira, you are the baby girl. Why do you act like the whole family is your responsibility? Well, newsflash, they aren't. You are in a worry-free zone this entire weekend. I mean, that is what it is for. As long as I have known you, you always act like the mother and not the child. Have some fun tonight, get loose, and get silly. Shoot, you can preach to your neighbor how good God is, but you're going out, we will have fun, and you must wear that dress. Now I can do your hair and makeup and we can be off," Mariah preached as she ran to get supplies to fix Semira's hair.

In no less than forty-five minutes, Semira was transformed and gorgeous. She had to admit, Mariah did an impeccable job. She was high stepping. However, what Mariah failed to understand was that Semira had to be responsible as did Seth. Their household and upbringing were completely different than hers.

Semira didn't argue with her, but before they left, Semira called Nalani to say good night. Nalani told her she loved her and she said the same.

"Semira, come on. It's getting late and I want to eat at the buffet," Mariah yelled from downstairs.

"I'm coming, I'm coming, and I'm here," Semira huffed with a smile as she followed her out the door and got into her Infiniti QX56. Semira liked to drive so she could leave when she wanted. Most times Mariah would protest, but she went along with it. They arrived at the club before too long, and Semira hoped that the food was still available so Mariah wouldn't be upset. The line was getting longer by the minute. They parked in VIP and walked past everyone. Semira heard the other females, say "who they think they are," and Mariah, being true to who she is, turned and replied, "We are VIP, and you would be?" That silenced them, and they walked right in. Semira liked that.

The chicken wings smelled so good, but Semira was still full from her Momma's house, so she just got cranberry juice— no vodka, just juice. They sat down at an empty table, but it was not empty for long because the basketball team was coming in. They had won a game so the place was full of energy. Semira saw Mariah trying to eat quickly before the guys sat down and she laughed out loud.

Before she knew it, VIP was surrounded by tall handsome athletes and typical chicken heads and jump offs. Semira looked at Mariah and told her she was going to the dance floor, and she followed. As they walked by, one of the guys grabbed Mariah's arm, and she jerked it back. Semira shook her head. He had no idea what he was about to unleash.

"Can I help you with something?" Mariah snapped. Her index finger was ready for action. She had taken the guy by surprise. He tried to be suave and slick. He winked and got closer to her.

"I just want to know what a lovely lady like you is doing without a man."

"Well, what makes you think I don't have one?" She countered as she placed her hands on her hips, her neck was rolling from one side to the other. Semira stood back in silence. Mariah was going to chew him up and spit him out.

"I just assumed that—"

Mariah put up her hands to shut him up. She shook her head; he had opened the door, and on top of that, he looked an absolute hot mess, and then some. Mariah shifted her body weight and snapped her neck as she responded, "You should never assume because when you do, you make an ass out of yourself and you make me have to be one to you, so chill with that."

Sermira dropped her head because she knew her girl didn't mind cursing a dude out. At least the word she used was in the Bible.

The guy frowned, but he dared not say anything else and stood aside for them to pass. They finally made it to the dance floor. It wasn't really crowded so Semira convinced Mariah to do their party stroll. Though they were part of the graduate chapter of their sorority, they still were young ones and wanted to show off a little. They were out there doing their thing and having a good time when some guys came to the floor. That was Semira's cue to leave. They were cute, but not her type. To be honest, she was not sure what her type was anymore. She didn't want any man grinding on her or touching her body. It was just an unpleasant invasion that she didn't want. It made her feel dirty. She liked to dance but she just didn't like to be ground on. She could see that Mariah was feeling them, so she eased out of sight and watched her. She was having a ball. As Semira turned to walk to the bar, someone grabbed her hand. She figured it was Mariah so she didn't turn around right away, but she just kept walking. Then the grip got stronger and the person gently pulled her back. She turned around. "Excuse me but who do you think you are?" she inquired.

"It's me. Ajani. Se Se, why are you acting like that?" he asked, a little offended.

She stopped and stared for a moment. He was more filled out. She had not seen him since high school. He was one of the few good ones. "Oh, well give me a hug. How are you doing?" she shouted above the music and feeling a little badly for not noticing him sooner. He was a nice guy from what she remembered.

"I'm doing well, and yourself?" He smiled.

"I'm doing great too. I'm so glad to see you," she replied politely.

"You look real nice in that dress. Real nice."

Semira playfully poked him. "You are doing way too much looking. So how is Cherie doing? Are you married yet?"

she asked moving out of the way of the constant flow of traffic that was coming. People seemed to lose their manners when they are in a club like they can't *"say excuse me or nothing."*

"Oh man, Cherie and I are separated for the time being. You know she wants to be an actress and live in big city Hollywood, but I'm content being a country boy."

She nodded. "I don't mean to be rude, but I have to go get something to drink. I will catch up with you later, like at church or something," she shouted over the music. He nodded and she disappeared into the crowd.

4. Deonna

Chapter 4

She ordered her water and went back to the table to sit down and catch her breath, but she was not alone for long.

"Hey there, Miss Lady. How are you doing?" a soothing, soft baritone voice inquired.

Semira looked up expecting to give the guy a hard time, but when she saw him, she was speechless. She wondered if she were still dizzy because the man in front of her was as fine as they come. His momma and daddy had created a work of art. Semira had to get herself together. "Are you speaking to me?" she queried shyly as she looked around thinking he was talking to someone else. He was looking much too handsome to be in a club surfing for women.

"Yes, I saw you earlier but you and your friend walked by quickly. I'm sure I have not seen you here before. Excuse me if I'm too forward, but what's your name?"

What is my name? she thought to herself as she gawked at him. His hair was the tint of black sand, his skin the color of Caribbean lands, his eyes were rare green, a shade she had never seen on another man, and he smelled like Burberry. He left her in awe for a moment, but Semira acted as if she wasn't fazed. "My name is Semira," she replied as she sipped her water. She noticed him. She took notice, but she was not about to feed his ego tonight. Her mind knew how fine men with ego boosters acted. He did remind her of a past love.

"It is a pleasure to meet you, Semira, and my name is Carmine." He smiled at her. "May I have a seat?"

"Sure." She moved her jacket and allowed him to sit. She didn't make much eye contact. She was wondering where Mariah had gone to. She was much better with guys than Semira was. For some reason, she instantly felt like a school girl, wondering to herself what this fine man found so tempting about her. She was really not that interesting and she found it difficult to have a conversation with a man if it had nothing to do with work. She was just uncomfortable and she didn't trust men, especially ones that approached in clubs and were athletes. Clubs were not the place to meet Mr. Right. At least, that was her philosophy. Besides, she was not looking. She wished she had stayed home and went over some finance stuff and read up on the new tax law. Instead, she was sitting and feeling awkward with this fine guy staring at her like he'd never seen a woman before. Was she sending off some kind of vibe? If so, she would gladly turn it off.

"Semira is a beautiful name. It is unique and I like things that are unique," he complimented after a three-minute pause. Her eyes shimmered from the light. She was definitely a beauty.

4. Deonna

Semira almost choked on her water. She hated men who used pickup lines. *How lame do you have to be for some stuff like that?* He was losing points already, not that it even mattered because she was not interested in getting to know him.

"Well, my name is African. It means 'fulfilled,'" she educated him. "Oh, and it is nice to meet you as well, Carmine." She was trying to be polite. She was so out of her element that every word she said sounded like an insult. This was why she never dated. She just didn't have that flow, but if they had been talking about numbers, his financial portfolio, the stock market, or anything dealing with money, she was on it, but not this small talk. She felt it was a waste; say what you want to say, and don't go fishing, just spit it out.

He was quiet for a moment, trying to decide how to take her. He definitely was not used to a woman giving him a hard time, but he found he liked the challenge. Some things were worth the effort. "So, what are you doing here in VIP?" he asked, intrigued by her and mesmerized by her outfit. She showed just enough to leave you yearning for more.

She figured he asked her that because she wasn't a jump-off, a video vixen, model or socialite. She was just a plain Jane doing her best not to be noticed. "My friend knows the owner of the club. He likes her so she can do pretty much what she wants," Semira stated, wondering what he was getting at.

"Oh okay. I only asked because I must say that you are one of the most tasteful women I have met here. Usually, these women in here try to find the man with the money and dig him dry, but you and your girl got the guys digging. I find that attractive."

Semira saw him checking her out. He was so obvious. "Carmine, please don't get offended by what I'm going to say, but if you are looking for a one night stand or a quickie, I'm not the woman for you. I'm not impressed by stats or the amount of money you have in your bank account. I don't do ego. If that is what you are seeking, then I'm not the woman for you. I'm simply here because my friend made me come. I'm not into having some man come up to me throw me a line like I'm a fish, and when he thinks he has me hooked, tries to reel me in with sweet talk. That isn't how I get down. I just thought I would let you know before you waste any more of my time, as well as yours." Semira wasn't trying to be rude, but she was not in the mood for his sweet talking. That was how her sister got in trouble, believing every lie a man told her. Her momma too, with Samson, because a man will sing any song to get what he wanted, and then the real man appeared and she was not about to be another notch in his belt. She knew better than that. He must have thought he was talking to some insecure chick looking for a handout. It wasn't her. She had her own a long time ago, man free.

He hadn't been expecting that. Never had that ever happened in his life, but this one here came with guns blazing and it made him wonder who'd hurt her. She was all kinds of salty. "Ouch! You're more like a jellyfish. You know how to sting with your words. It is obvious you are not in the mood for conversation so I won't interrupt you any longer, but you are wrong about me." He stood to leave and she acted like he was already gone, but before his foot could move, Mariah popped up.

"Semira, who is your fine friend?" Mariah inquired as she prevented the hotness from leaving.

Semira looked at him with the side eye and then at her. "This is Carmine, but I think he was about to leave." Semira was offended that he thought because he was handsome and giving her attention that she was going to be eating out of his hands. *Please*. He needed to come better than that. She wasn't some uneducated, star gazing girl. She was good and grown. She had plenty of men checking for her and she turned them down. She already knew the game and was not interested in playing.

Mariah ignored her friend. "Nonsense, Carmine, you sit right back down and don't pay Semira any attention. Sometimes she leaves her manners at home. So how are you?" Mariah asked, quickly engaging him in conversation. She knew for a fact that Semira could be rude. It was her defense mechanism.

This dismissal of her feelings upset Semira. Mariah had no right to intervene on her behalf. She said what she meant, and she meant what she said. She didn't need anyone explaining away her attitude or her mood.

Mariah kicked Semira under the table and gave her the eye. So Semira decided to play nice. "Sorry, Carmine, I didn't mean to be rude, but you have to understand when we come into places like this, we always meet flies," she responded honestly.

He looked at her, wondering what being a fly referred to. "What's a fly?" he cautiously and curiously asked.

Semira looked at Mariah and they laughed at each other. "It is a man who is full of stink, to be nice about it. Basically, a fly will land on anything if you get my drift," Semira explained. She was a Christian woman, and she didn't want to use profanity so she hoped he got her meaning. Truly, she shouldn't be in a place like this. She could have been preparing for her Sunday school class, or watching a movie and eating popcorn and brownies, anything but being here and dealing with flies.

He began to laugh as well. "I understand, but like I said before, you are wrong about me. I'm here with my friends too,

4. Deonna

and to be honest, I'm not that big on clubs. It is just that my friend and I have been hitting the scene trying to meet people."

Semira nodded her head. Mariah decided that three was a crowd and left the table. Semira sat there wishing Mariah had let him leave. This was not Semira's strong suit and worst of all, she had nothing to talk about, nothing that would probably be of interest to him. This was going from bad to worse.

"So, Semira, do you like basketball?"

She shrugged her shoulders. It was not like she was a die-hard fan, but she comprehended the game. "No, not really. I mean I can watch it, but I like football and baseball better," she replied as she turned toward him. She and Mariah went to every home game and sometimes they traveled to the away games, depending on her schedule. Mr. Calloway always made sure they had a good time. "What about you?" she asked, sipping the rest of her water.

He leaned in closer. He inhaled her delicious scent, a blend of lavender and lilac, and it smelled so good on her. "I like a little of everything. Since I play basketball, it is my favorite sport." He grinned.

Oops, she thought to herself. Maybe her saying that hurt his feelings. He said his name was Carmine, but she had no idea who he was. She wondered if he played for Carolina. He must have been new because she didn't recall him. "Oh, so you got traded?"

"I thought you weren't a basketball fan?"

She smiled. "I'm not, but I know about my home team. I do go to a game here and there, but I never saw you. Last season was rough for the team, so I haven't been to a game this season."

"Yeah, I got traded from Miami," he said.

Semira nodded her head in disbelief. "Really? That's too bad. Miami is a much better team. Our team won't see the playoffs until like five years from now, if that. You might want to rethink that one," she counseled. She wondered why he got traded, but then it was the NBA and they didn't care about trading their players. She wondered who his agent was or if he were a free agent because if he needed some new representation, she had some connection in the sports world and would be willing to assist him.

He was surprised by her brutal honesty. "You are a harsh woman. You know a lot about basketball not to watch it. I like you, though. You certainly speak your mind, and hold no punches."

"I'm sorry. I just haven't been out in forever, so you have to overlook me when I talk too much," she explained, mentally slapping herself. It was how she operated, though. She had to beat the man before the man could beat her.

"You are forgiven. I don't hold grudges. Why have you not been out in so long?"

"Thanks. I just have a lot on my plate, so having a night out on the town is hard with work and everything else," she replied.

He scooted closer to her. She could not help but notice how good he smelled, a wonderful serenade to her senses. She tried to not act impressed, but in all honesty, her heart was leaping out of her chest. This fine man was all on her, he was a basketball player, and he talked like he had sense. On top of that, the man had good taste. They were actually having a real conversation in a club, and even though VIP was bumping it was like they were alone. "So what made your momma name you Carmine?" He looked at her like "why, is she going to trip on my name?"

"I'm asking because I like it. It's Italian right?" she asked as she adjusted in her seat to get more comfortable.

He smiled at me and gave her a wink. "Yes, it is Italian. My father is Sicilian and my mother is African American.

"Oh okay. I wasn't trying to dig into your family heritage. I just like Carmine. Anyway, how do you like the south? I know North Carolina is different from Florida. I'm kind of wondering did you get signed from somewhere else because I didn't know Miami had an Italian community." Well, she didn't really know anyone in Miami, but she and Mariah went once and it was great. A little too much for Semira but it was a good time. The Brown and Black brothers were wonderful eye candy. She got eye cavities from seeing all the fineness. She'd do it all again. The memory made her smile.

"I attended college in Miami, but I lived in New Jersey. You are right about that, it's not a large community but we're there, but I also like it here. Especially the accents you all have," he teased, smiling and impressed that she said what she thought and didn't seem to be shy.

Semira nodded my head. She was quiet. She never liked it when people commented on southern accents. They always wanted to make southern folks sound like they were silly when they sounded just as funny. Most people judged the south by the way people spoke as if they were ignorant, but that was far from the truth. Semira stopped the waitress as she passed by the table. "Excuse me miss, may I have a Sierra Mist cranberry?" The waitress nodded and walked toward the bar.

"You don't drink?" he observed, leaning closer to converse with her. This one here really was different.

"Nah, alcohol isn't my friend. I can't handle it, so I leave it alone." On a dare one night, she drank a six pack of

4. Deonna

Corona and let's just say she learned her lesson. She stood up to stretch her legs. It was after midnight and she was ready to go home. She started yawning. "Excuse me. I've gotten sleepy. I don't think I'm ready for these all night clubbing weekends. I need to be in bed," she said, laughing. That was probably more than he wanted to know.

He started to laugh as well. "How old are you?"

She looked at him for a moment. Now didn't he know that it was rude to ask a lady her age? "I'm twenty-five. Why?"

He realized he may have offended her by the cold gaze she was giving him and that extra attitude. "I'm twenty-seven and you act older than me. You're young and are supposed to be out here having a good time."

Who was he? Good looking, yes, but being fine didn't give him the right to offer his unsolicited advice. "I can have a great time curled in my bed with a Sudoku puzzle, reading *The Economist*." She sat back down. He had the most alluring eyes. She found herself staring for a moment. He was irritating and handsome all at once. He had her twisted, but she would never confess that out loud. Soon the waitress brought her drink, and she sipped it.

"You know, if you are sleepy you should have gotten something with caffeine in it," he suggested.

He must have never had a Sierra Mist cranberry, because it always gave her a boost. They talked a little longer and Mariah finally came back for Semira. She told Carmine goodnight and left the club. Semira was happy to get out of there. His eyes were bewitching and slowly she felt herself succumbing to them. It was foolish. She quickly regained her senses. She knew better. She shut love down a long time ago, and for good reason. Love was risky and it was no longer something that she actively sought. Her niece and her nephew were more than enough for her.

"Semira, I'm going to tell your momma. You just had perfection all over you and you dismissed dude. He was *fine, fine*, and then some more *fine*! What are you doing?" she scolded, baffled by her friend's behavior.

Semira shook her head, somewhat annoyed by her chatter. She knew why and that was all. Semira didn't owe anyone an explanation. "Nothing. I'm doing nothing," she snapped, frustrated. He was not the first one to flirt with her. She dealt with athletes, agents, and businessmen all the time, but she didn't want to date anyone. That was trouble. Plus, she had some unresolved issues that she was working out. Besides, she was not about to open her home, heart, nor her niece to that kind of stupidity. She knew his kind and his type. She was better off single. There was nothing wrong with being without a man. Most women who had one were either in misery, paranoid or just settled. That was not the kind of example she was going to set for Nalani. There were too many responsibilities for her to act footloose and fancy-free.

"Exactly! Do something! Get that man. He is feeling you. I saw Ajani and he told me you blew him off too. Why? He is single," she exclaimed.

"I didn't blow him off. He's separated. Besides, I was thirsty and he was not coming between me and H2O so tell him to deal with it. I talked to Carmine and was friendly, but I have Nalani to think about. I don't have time for a man right now. I hardly have time for me," Semira quipped as she got into the car. She drove right to the Waffle House because she was hungry. This used to be their hangout in college. Once inside, they sat and Mariah kept on and on. Semira begged them to rush her order. Finally, the food came and Mariah's lips hushed, but only momentarily.

"You know, Semira, I think you're using Nalani as an excuse because you are scared. That little girl needs a good male role model as much as you need a boyfriend," Mariah demanded. Then she hit the table like she thought of something. "Semira, this is about Natano, isn't it?"

Semira's eyes widened with shock. Mariah was going in on her all because of some dude in the club. Why would she even bring up Natano? That was a wound still fresh. She knew Mariah didn't know the full story. If she had, she would not have said his name. Semira decided to ignore the latter part and only address the first part. "Look, that Carmine is a basketball player, which means he is a playa. He probably goes through women like he does shoes. I'm not about to give a man like that an opportunity to use and abuse me. Oh no, my sister girl. You know how I feel about relationships. It's like women get stupid when they get a man. I'm not about that life."

Mariah stretched her eyes at Semira trying to get her to hush, but she was on a roll.

"I'm telling the truth. Look at the athletes, rappers, and actors all caught up in these sex scandals with a million baby mamas. It's like they're sex freaks and have sexual addictions. *'How many women I can get.'* I don't think so." Semira was deep into the conversation that she lifted her fork to nail home the last part of her mini sermon.

"Semira, please hush," Mariah calmly warned.

"Why?" Then she pointed her finger and Semira looked behind her and Carmine and his get along gang were standing behind her. Why were millionaire players at the local Waffle House? Had they followed them? She smiled at him and turned back around. She looked at Mariah and saw that her friend was embarrassed which made Semira wonder how long Carmine had been present. She turned back around and asked. "How long you been standing there?"

"Not long." He smiled. "May we join you?"

Semira was like, *not again.* She wanted to sit here, eat, talk mess, burp and pass gas if necessary. All the things a lady did when she was with her sister girl, but she guessed she would have to hold her gas. "Be my guest," she forced herself to say. They sat down. "So who are you?" she asked the guy who was with Carmine.

"My name is Leon."

"Nice to meet you, Leon, this is Mariah, and I'm Semira," she replied with a smile. Mariah was glowing. She loved her men dark and lovely. He was every bit that. They talked and Semira ate. "Look at the time." She looked down at her watch. It was going on three in the morning. "Mariah, we need to be going. I have a lot to do tomorrow."

Mariah looked at Semira like she had lost her mind. "Okay, well, guys it was nice to meet you all. Hopefully, we will see you all again." She nodded in agreement.

"Hold on," Carmine requested as she was getting her purse.

"What?" she asked half perplexed.

"Semira, I would like to call you sometime. May I have your number?"

Semira thought for a second. "Are you sure, because I can't stand for a man to ask for my number and never use it. Don't ask me to take the time to give it and you don't use it."

Mariah shook her head. She couldn't take Semira anywhere. For a Christian woman, she sure was harsh, mean and judgmental. That had been her mode since Sophina got pregnant with Nalani.

Carmine smiled again at her. "May I have your number?"

Semira reluctantly gave it to him. She grabbed the bill and went to pay. He followed. "You don't have to pay for us. We're gentlemen," he told her seriously.

"I know I don't have to, but I will. I don't mind. I got my own money," she responded, gave the cashier the bill, and they all walked out together. She wanted to let him know that she was not looking to be taken care of. She was more than capable of taking care of herself. She worked hard for her money and was raising her niece the same way. All a woman needed was God because He was a necessity. Anything else was just an accessory. She had enough of those already. She wanted to let him know she was not like the other women he had met. In the words of Jamie Foxx and Ne-Yo, "she got her own."

4. Deonna

Chapter 5

The next morning Semira felt that kind of tired you get when you are too old to be hanging out all night at clubs. It was good that Nalani had spent the night with her G-Momma. She would have had her up before sunrise, dragging her to see cartoons and making her blackberry waffles. Her baby was different. She didn't like blueberries, but she loved blackberries.

Semira forced herself to go to the bathroom and soak her body in a tub of hot water. The hot water felt good on her cold skin. She let herself relax a little while longer before she started her day. She closed her eyes, thought about Carmine, and listed all the reasons why they were not meant for one another, but for some annoying reason, the thought of him made her smile and that scared her. Dating was not an option right now. Shoot, dating was never an option. She had to keep her guard up and not let herself get lost in the temptation of him. The reason she avoided social places was because she wanted to keep those feelings of lust, infatuation, and longing at bay, far from her. Now, for some reason, Carmine had somehow infiltrated her mind. That made her furious. She got out of the tub and dried off her wet body, contemplating what to do with the rest of her day. In order to occupy her mind, she decided to go the mall and shop for some new clothes. Before going, she stopped by

Mariah's house first to see what she was up to. "Mariah, are you busy?" she asked as she walked into her home

"No, come on in this house. It's windy outside. So what brings you out?" Mariah asked, wearing a big smile like she was searching Semira for information.

"I'm headed to the mall, and I wanted to know if you'd go with me," she replied as Mariah's Bengal cat jumped into her arms. Semira was terribly afraid of domestic cats, but for some reason Mariah's cat loved her, so she pretended.

"Of course, you need me to help you find the right outfit because I know Carmine will be asking you out," her sultry voice hummed and she smiled at Semira before taking Benny out of her arms.

"Oh, hush up with that mess. I'm not bothered!" Semira lied. A part of her wanted his company. That feeling was frightening to her because it was new. She was well aware of how dangerous letting her guard down could be.

"I bet he won't even call and I won't even care. I'm telling you, he is too fine to be a one-woman man. He is an NBA player and I'm me. I'm not famous. I'm not a millionaire. I'm no supermodel and I have no ambition to be a jump-off. So what interest would he have in me? I'm just being real," Semira quipped, rolled her eyes, and let out a deep breath. The discussion was getting on her nerves.

4. Deonna

"See, that is the attitude that keeps you single. You're intelligent. You're hard working, and you're a strong, independent, caring Christian woman who would give her life to help another in need. You may not be Oprah, but you are comfortable. Believe me, that is what that man sees in you. It's your inner beauty plus your outer beauty that attracts men. I know you, girl. I'm your best friend. It doesn't hurt that you got a tight butt and a beautiful face." Seeing that her friend was contemplating what she was saying, Maria kept talking. "You know, successful men like successful women." In Semira's case, most men who attempted to ask her out failed, epically. Now this basketball player was trying and probably would fail too. Men loved Semira but she refused to allow herself to love them back, all because of Natano. It was time for her to get over him. Being bitter wasn't cute.

Semira smiled at her. She always knew how to pick her up. Thank God for good friends like that. "Whatever, come on so we can shop and go out to eat."

"Se Se, have you heard from Sophina yet?"

"No, not yet. I haven't heard from her in a while. She was calling every Saturday up until a year ago. I don't know if Dante has her all caught up or what, but something isn't right. I just worry, you know." Semira shook her head.

"I know you do, but your sister is twenty-seven years old. She knows better. She is aware of what she is doing. She has to take responsibility for her actions. Your whole family has bent over backwards for her. It is time for her to do something," Mariah fussed.

That was the truth. Semira knew Mariah was right. She agreed, but it was a subject she didn't want to linger on. "So did you meet any guys at the club last night?" she asked skeptically.

"Not really. I mean Leon was yummy but you know how I am. I like to flirt. I'm kind of feeling Duane. I know he likes me too, but you know he wants commitment. I don't know if I can do that yet."

Semira gave her the side eye. See folks loved to give advice but hated to accept it. Mariah was a prime example. "Mariah, Duane is wonderful. He cares about you. He would do anything you ask. I think it is about time you stop flirting and start loving. He may be the man God put on this earth for you. Try it!" she encouraged. She actually liked Duane for her friend. The man had it going on. He was a handsome, dark skinned brother, intelligent, kind, a pillar of the community and well financed. He had that good FICO score.

"You are one to talk. You have dismissed every good looking guy that has tried to talk to you. I mean you can find everything wrong with a man," Mariah replied, shaking her head.

Good looking doesn't mean he's a good man. "That isn't true. My bio-father is handsome and you see he wasn't good. Anyway, help me find these jeans in a size eight. You know you wrong for that. I just dismiss the ones that need to be," she replied and stuck out her tongue, acting more like Nalani than an adult.

"See, you need more adult time. That is what Nalani would do. We need to go out more. What are you doing tonight?" she asked purposely, ignoring the comment about Samson.

"I have a date."

Mariah lifted up an eyebrow and completely stopped what she was doing. Her girl was holding out. "With who, thank you, Lord, tell me who?" she asked. "Did Blaine finally ask you out? He is some kind of fine for white chocolate."

"Mariah, now you know he's like my brother. Actually, I think he should ask you out. As for me, I have a date with *Lockup*. You know that is my show. I don't go anywhere until after eleven o'clock at night. I have to see my show," Semira replied, super serious. She'd loved that show since it started and she never missed an episode.

Mariah burst into hysterical laughter and ignored the suggestion that she and Blaine should date. That was never happening.

"Stop laughing at me," Semira demanded.

"I'm sorry. C'mon, let's eat. We need some food."

Semira followed her out of the store and they ate at the Pasta Grill. As she was about to take a bite of her food, her cell phone started to ring. She picked it up and it was Nalani. She looked at Mariah and her eyes grew with excitement. She shook her head, whispered Nalani, and her smile semi-faded.

"Hey, sweetheart, I have your clothes and I will bring them to you in a little while."

"No, Auntie Se Se. I was calling because Uncle Seth is taking Tobias to go ice skating at the lake and I want to go too."

"That is fine with me. Let me talk to Seth real fast." Semira heard her scream for Seth and then pass him the phone. She got so tickled.

"Hey there, Sis. How are you doing?"

"I'm great. Look, I told Nalani it is fine if she wants to go. Does she need anything?" Semira asked her brother.

"No, I got this one. Sophina called me this morning," he whispered. He didn't want the children to hear.

That was a complete shock to her. "Well, how is she doing?" Semira questioned, wondering why she'd called Seth.

71

4. Deonna

He sighed. "She needs money. I told her that I didn't have any. She didn't even talk to Nalani. I just hope she is all right."

Semira could hear the stress in his voice. He was the big brother and couldn't do anything for her. That hurt him most of all. He could not understand.

"Seth, I'm sure she is fine. If she is calling for money, then she's okay. Don't tell Nalani about it. Just let her have a good time. She deserves that. She isn't to eat too many sweets." Then she hung up the phone. She looked at Mariah who knew what the conversation had been about. "Well, Seth is taking the kids to the lake to skate. Nalani is excited about it," Semira said, smiling.

"Semira, we should go to the game tonight," Mariah said, reading her friend's eyes and worrying about her.

"What? Why? We just went out yesterday. I'm not that big of a basketball fan," she protested. She liked football and she loved it since growing up watching Seth play and then Natano. It got her hyped, but basketball was not as exciting.

"Oh hush up, you love sports and you know it. Stop allowing your sister's mishaps to be your excuse. Have some fun. Nalani will be fine. Let's get our nails and hair done. We'll wear some cute outfits and have a good time. The game starts in a few hours. It's one o'clock now. We can be out of here by five o'clock."

Even when she didn't want to do something, Mariah had a way of making her want to. Maybe somewhere inside, a part of her did want too. "Okay, I will bite. We should have some fun."

Mariah grinned, and they hopped up and started to get fabulous.

As they entered the salon, the smell of hair was all over. It hit the pit of Semira's stomach but ignoring the feeling, they both entered the chair at the same time. Each told their stylist what they wanted and added that they had to be out before five o'clock in order to have time to bathe and put on makeup. Semira actually enjoyed being spoiled for a change. She had been keeping Nalani for so long, she had forgotten how to take care of herself. She leaned back and enjoyed the moment. Before she knew it, their princess power hour was over and they were walking to the car. Semira could see the heads turning and she had to admit she liked being the center of attention. It was a blessing that Nalani wanted to spend the weekend with her cousin. Semira got into Mariah's car and they drove to Semira's house. As soon as they got there, Semira checked her messages just to see if Sophina had called her, but she hadn't. Semira guessed in a small way she was grateful. She hopped into the shower and then brushed her teeth. When she walked out, Mariah was gleaming. "Girl, why are you so happy?" Semira queried as she started to put on her jewelry.

"Guess who just called your cell phone?" She beamed like she had won the Miss America pageant.

"Who is it?" Semira asked, half annoyed.

"Guess!!" she demanded, her eyes sparkling with enchantment. She was even running in place which made Semira laugh.

"Was it Carmine?"

"Yes!" She shrieked at the top of her lungs. "He invited us to the game tonight. I told him we were already coming, so he said he would make sure we had floor seats. He wanted to talk to you, but you know you were busy. He asked me if you would go out with him after the game and I told him you would." She was smiling even more.

"You did what? Why must you and my mother always play cupid? I don't want to go out on a date. I haven't been on a date since, well it doesn't matter."

"Since we were in Jr. High and that does not count because it was a group date, and your brother had to come. Now, you are going. So put on those jeans that make your butt look good and that black silk camisole top that makes your breasts look good."

Semira stood there in awe. That was untrue. Natano and she had gone out. She just didn't tell her. Anyway, had she not heard one word that Semira said. Had she been talking to herself? She walked to her bedroom and put the outfit together, but she decided she liked the ivory top better. It covered. She put on her ivory boots and she looked good. "Do you like this outfit, Mariah?" Semira asked her as she was putting the finishing touch on her outfit.

"You look good. Do those little spins so I can get the whole effect?"

Semira turned around and Mariah screamed. "That's scandalous, and I love it. Make sure he sees the back of that shirt. You are rocking that winter white like nobody has ever seen. I want to change outfits," she complained.

"Oh no, we're going. Come on so we can get a good parking place. Call Carmine back to make sure he will have the tickets because I look too good not to be seen," Semira reminded, pretending like she was not nervous. She was. She was so scared and hoped she didn't say or do anything stupid. The last date she had been on was in her freshman year, and he was the hottest guy she had ever seen, Natano. He was from California, a fine Samoan, tall, well-built and just cool. He was fine in every essence of the word and he made Carmine look like SpongeBob. As hard as she tried to deny it, she was madly in love with him, until Sophina ruined him. All she knew was that she'd loved him like she had loved no one else and trusted him instantly, and he'd chosen Sophina. No man was going to ever equal Natano.

Her sister took him, used him for his finances, and got pregnant by him and dumped him. He never knew about Nalani, only Sophina and Semira knew the truth. Their sisterly secret. She guessed that was why she loved Nalani so much because she was the daughter she would never have, by the only man she ever loved. Natano was who she missed. No other man was going to be able to really connect with her because of him, and the things left unsaid. If only Sophina would have allowed Semira to have that one piece of happiness, but she destroyed all hope of love ever finding Semira. Semira let her. She accepted defeat without fighting because the betrayal was too much. Now, even as old as she was, the hurt from that still mocked her. Sophina was living her life while Semira was still cleaning up behind her.

"What? That is the attitude I like to hear."

Mariah's voice brought Semira back to reality. Now she was going to have to fake it until she could make it. That seemed to be her motto. She just always hid how she truly felt. Who'd care anyway? She got into Mariah's car and they headed toward the destination. Semira called Carmine and he assured her that he had left them some tickets, and to just ask. He sounded really sweet on the phone, and he wanted to let her know that he did call her so she couldn't give him a hard time. He also asked her out after the game. She hesitated, but accepted. There was no reason to turn down a free meal. She remembered Mariah saying that.

When they got there, it was getting crowded. Mariah parked and Semira walked to get their tickets. There was no problem. Once Mariah met her, they went to find an usher so he could show them where to go. Carmine really did hook them up with great seats. They were directly behind the team. Semira could actually touch Carmine if she wanted.

"Semira, you make it work with this man. Girl, we can meet celebrities, have seats this close to the floor and go on luxurious vacations. I think I like Carmine. Please be nice to him. The guy is trying to impress you," Mariah said, looking around the arena. She was excited for Semira.

Semira nodded as Mariah talked. "You know I'm hungry," Semira complained as her stomach growled loudly.

"Don't eat too much. The man is taking you out," Mariah warned.

"Oh, yeah, I guess I can wait," Semira acquiesced, leaning back in her chair and watching the auditorium fill up with people. Finally, the guys came out to warm up. Semira spotted Carmine. He was number one. "Look, girl, his number is one. I'm telling you that man is cocky," Semira judged, folding her arms disapprovingly.

Mariah shook her head, annoyed at her friend's behavior. She had no clue why Se Se was being so hateful about Carmine and it made her wonder if she was secretly feeling him. "Semira, stop being so judgmental. Why are you already trying to find something wrong with him? You supposed to be a Christian and there you go jumping to assumptions. What I told you about assuming?" Mariah fussed, looking annoyed at Semira.

Mariah's reactions somewhat stunned Semira, but she didn't reply. In truth, Mariah was right about calling her out, but she needed to understand Semira's point of view. If she found something wrong now, then she would not be so heartbroken when he cheated, lied, or mistreated her. It was better to go into the situation with armor and be ready for battle than to be blindsided. She was just preparing herself for the end. Carmine noticed her, winked, and gave her a brief smile. Semira blushed and prayed that the cameras didn't catch him. Mariah jabbed her side. So when he looked again, Semira smiled. "Mariah, you got one more time to jab me and I'm going to get unchristian-like on you," Semira snapped, annoyed. Mariah was really getting on Semira's nerves, hitting her each time she didn't like something she said or did as it pertained to Carmine. Just because Semira kept her mouth shut didn't mean she couldn't get wild too. People always presumed her meekness was a sign of weakness, but that was untrue. She grew up in violence so she didn't like it, but she could hold her own when necessary.

"Sorry, but you know how you are," she amended, looking innocently at her friend, whose facial expression revealed her dismay.

The guys got into a huddle, did their little routine, and went to their seats. Semira had never seen so many fine men in one place. The guys may not have been the best team, but they were the best looking. Carmine looked different in uniform. She watched as they got into position and noted that he was the point guard.

"Mariah, you know he used to play for Miami. Now, he is competing against them. I hope our guys win this one."

Mariah nodded in agreement.

The first half was uneventful so Semira went to the restroom. The team was getting slapped. Then it was like something happened and the boys started to make a comeback, but one of the guys fouled Leon, and before Semira knew it, she was standing up and shouting. Mariah pulled her back down and began to laugh at her. By the second half, they were down

4. Deonna

by eight points, and Semira was into it. She was screaming and shouting, and fussing.

"Mariah, I like this. We should do it more often," Semira suggested.

Mariah was smiling at her because she was so controlled. The last time Mariah recalled her best friend cutting loose like this was their senior year in high school. It was nice for a change. Semira was feeling it. "*Swoosh.*" Carmine made a three-pointer. Finally, he was making progress over his old team. It was the last quarter and the home team was down five points. "*Swoosh.*" Carmine made another three, and Semira was on the edge of her seat with her fingers crossed. The team called a time out. They were up one and there were only two minutes left in the game, which meant they could still lose. The game resumed and both teams were playing hard. Semira watched the clock. Shake, the small forward threw the ball and missed. Leon got the rebound and gave it to Carmine who went for a lay-up—two points. Now there was a minute left. Carmine's team was up three points. Shake made a three-pointer. Now everyone, fans and players alike, were standing but not speaking as the clock counted down. Semira could feel it. She knew they would win. Leon dribbled the ball, but number seven stole it from him, made a two-pointer at the buzzer, and Miami won. Semira felt sorry for the guys, but this was the best they had played since they had started. The last game they won had been a fluke. This one was really good. She looked at Mariah, who was flirting with the point guard from the other team, so Semira jabbed her.

"Girl, come back to reality. You're so naughty," Semira fussed, shocked by her friend's lack of loyalty.

"It was all in harmless fun. Come on, you need to comfort your boo thang."

"Hush-up, I most certainly will not. He isn't my boo thang, and I so hate that term. They just lost and I'm not going to mess with him. Besides, I need to freshen up. You know I can't look a hot mess," Semira replied, and they walked to the restroom so that Semira could reapply her make-up.

"Se Se, did he tell you where to meet him?" Mariah asked because she wanted everything to be perfect.

"No. I was thinking he might not want to go out anyway. I mean, you know with losing and all," Semira explained. She didn't mind if he canceled. She needed to take care of some business for work anyway. She liked getting an extra start. It made her customers feel special. This was about as much free time as she needed anyway.

Mariah rolled her eyes. Sometimes, Semira was so difficult to deal with. "Please, that brotha better get used to it.

4. Deonna

This team isn't made up of big ballas, and he needs to know that. However, he was hot tonight."

Semira nodded her head in agreement. Then her cell phone interrupted their conversation. "Hello?"

"Hey, Semira, this is Carmine. Where are you? I turned to look for you and you were gone." He wondered if she'd changed her mind about going out on a date. He was skipping the press tonight and just wanted to make a quick exit and not think about losing to a team he'd once played for.

"Oh, I had to use the restroom," she replied looking at Mariah, who was grinning from ear-to-ear.

"Well, will you come back? We can walk out the back exit," he requested.

"Um, okay. I will be back in a minute," she agreed, and then she began to talk to Mariah. "Are you coming with me?"

Mariah looked at Semira like she was stuck on stupid. For all her financial savvy swag, the girl was completely at a loss when it came to men and dating. "You go. Tell me everything that goes down, and if you need me to rescue you, just call. I think you will have a great time. Good luck, and for goodness sakes, please be nice," she urged as the two embraced.

Semira knew she needed to do it alone, but she felt stronger with Mariah by her side, and now she was going to be solo. She was panicked a little and then took a deep breath. She went back inside. Her heart was racing and her mind was telling her to retreat. She started to lose the little bit of confidence she'd just had. She stopped and took several deeper breaths to prevent having an anxiety attack. She started walking again and there was Carmine standing there waiting on her. He was glowing like an angel and looking oh so handsome. Semira walked up to him and smiled. "Good game," she greeted him.

"Thank you. So did you enjoy the seats?"

"I did, and thank you for that. That was really nice of you to hook us up. We both appreciated that a lot," she replied as she started to fidget with her hands. "So how did it feel to play your old team?"

"So you were listening to me last night?" he asked with a sly grin.

"I was." She smiled.

As they went through the exit door, he grabbed Semira's hand and pulled her close to his body. "We have some good fans, and some crazy ones, so stay close to me." All he needed was for her to get hurt on their first date. He didn't want to give her any reason to cut out early and not give him a fair chance at her heart.

For once in her life, she did as she was told and didn't give him attitude. There was a crowd that had gathered as well as cameras. She followed him to his SUV. He opened the door for her and she unlocked his door.

"Wow, that was massive. You deal with that a lot?" she asked as he got into the driver side.

"I'm used to it now," he told her as he closed his door. "Do you care what music I put in?"

"I listen to everything, but if it's a rap song I prefer the edited version. I don't like all that cursing and disrespecting women or talk about money, drinking and sex," she replied in a matter of fact way.

"I'm an old school brotha. I like jazz and oldies," he replied with a twinkle in his eye.

She couldn't believe he was the same guy she had given a hard time to yesterday, but the fact that he was willing to get to know her gave him some extra points. She was going to be in a no judge zone tonight and try to relax and have fun.

"So where are you taking me?" Semira asked, getting settled into the heated, leather seats.

He looked at her and turned down the music. "I'm taking you, madam, to this nice little Italian restaurant downtown. I love it. I made arrangements for them to open up tonight for us only." He was just glad she was still willing to go out with him. It was late and he had just lost the game to his old team, so he looked forward to spending this time with her.

She looked at him like he was crazy. How in the world could he just shut down a place just to eat? Interesting, she thought to herself. She sat back and listened to the music. He did have a great selection. A little Miles Davis, Louis Armstrong, Billie Holiday and Frank Sinatra. His taste reminded her of her stepfather's love for jazz music. She herself was a Nina Simone fan. He was racking up points.

Once they arrived, he opened the door for her and they walked into the restaurant. It was nice. The lights were dim and there were candles lit on the table. Their table was in the middle, and they were the only ones there dining. She was shocked he'd done that. No man had ever taken the time to go the extra mile for her. After she'd been a bit rude, he still showed how romantic and a gentleman he could be. He really shut it down. They were the only people dining.

"This is really refined. I like a man who has taste," she complimented, smiling on the inside but not showing her feelings on the outside. It would take more than that to impress her. She couldn't swoon now or he would flag her as easy.

He pulled out the chair for her. "Well thank you, ma'am. So, tell me about you. I can tell there is a lot of history in those big brown eyes. May I say you look beautiful in that outfit, very classy?" he complimented her.

4. Deonna

Semira felt her cheeks grow warm but quickly brought herself back. "Thank you. You look handsome as well," she replied as she sipped her water. "I don't know what to tell you about me. I need you to be more specific. You can ask me what you would like to know, and I will either be inclined to tell you, or I will decline. I will do the same to you. Does that sound fair?" This was not in line with her expertise. She hadn't been on a date of any kind since Natano.

He smirked a little. It was obvious that she was used to running things. He found that to be attractive. "That sounds fair to me. Why were you so harsh to me?" he asked.

She rolled her eyes playfully. "It has nothing to do with you. I'm like that to all men. I just saw some really bad things in my life as a result of men. It's in my best interest to be harsh, to protect myself and those I love," she pointedly replied. The truth was the truth. The only good men she had met were her brother, Seth and her stepfather, Josiah. Other than God, they were the only men she needed.

"Wow. So you had a bad relationship and you make every man put in the time for a crime he didn't commit?" he questioned, sitting upright and feeling like he'd figured her out. She was that kind of woman. Some dude broke her heart and made her bitter. She was the kind who had a chip on her shoulder and was a man hater. He should have seen that in the club, but she was so beautiful. It was easy to be drawn to her. He should have known it was too good to be true.

"See, you have me all wrong. Your presumption is very flawed. To be honest, I haven't had any relationships. They are in my mind, a waste of time," she quickly educated him. She stared right into his eyes, letting him know she spoke the truth. He was not as smooth or as smart as he thought. He knew nothing of her.

He looked stunned. "You are jerking my chain," he replied, wondering how else she could be so jaded. Someone had to do something for her to avoid dating and relationships.

"No," she answered honestly, as she moved her hair out of her face. "My biological father was really strict. Samson used to be very abusive to my mother and my siblings. Once he lost his job, it got worse. He was very hard on me and my siblings, but mostly on me. I think he hated me so much because I was the unplanned birth. Whatever reason it was, I just retreated to my own world. I read books, I wrote, I did every sport, every camp, anything to get away. When I was ten, my parents divorced and my mother began dating a new man. She got remarried, and we all call Josiah, Dad because he has always been so good to us. The damage Samson caused just made me become really suspect of all men. He was the greatest, and then he was the worst. He always found something to whoop me for.

4. Deonna

I used to get in trouble all the time because I did everything wrong or, at least, he said I did." She stopped. She had told this man her family history, a story only Mariah and her family knew. Why had she done that? The way he looked at her, with pity in his eyes made her regret opening her mouth.

Her truth was alarming to him. She spoke so direct as if it was a part of normal life. He felt so sorry to hear she had suffered so harshly, yet she seemed to not allow it to penetrate. "I'm sorry to hear that. I can see why you are so tough. I'm not a violent man. I do have a heart. I'm interested in knowing you. I can take it at your pace, but I do find you very interesting," he offered.

She smiled at him. "So, tell me about your last relationship," she asked, trying to move the conversation to something else other than herself.

"That ended two years ago. She was this cute Cuban chica I had met in college. We were friends forever. She couldn't handle me being a pro. She liked getting things, and being on the scene, but she didn't want to support me. It was like I give and she got, but she wasn't giving me anything. I had to drop her. My mother was not a fan of hers either. Then there were women coming out of the woodwork. My momma had told me to watch out because all that glimmers isn't gold. I remembered that. My momma is a God fearing woman as well.

She doesn't play. I tell you that to let you know I respect women. Being famous and having money has not changed me. I know that the talent I have is a gift from God, and that is how I treat it."

She smiled at him. He had won her over. A Christian man who loved his momma was number one on her list of what she needed in a man, but her dad had started out the same way. "You are full of surprises," was her response as she leaned back in her chair so she could get a better view of him. "So when did your passion for basketball start?"

As he was about to reply, the waiter brought out their salads. He lifted a questionable eyebrow as he took a bite of his salad.

She continued. "What I was saying was, I can tell you're passionate by how I saw you play. There are some players who are in it for the material things, the fame and the temporary things that it brings. It is like as a youth their dream was basketball and once that dream came true, they forgot the struggle, the beauty and the passion of the game. When I saw you play, it was real, like that was your love. It's not about winning for you, it's about being in the moment and doing what you love. You put in everything that is in you when you play, and the crowd can feel that. You have it in you to bring the purity back to the game. I admire that," she shared, and began to nibble on her salad.

He looked at her, speechless. It was his turn to lean back then forward then back again. His eyes widened and they were full of expression and longing to understand. "You…you could tell all that from one game?" Was this the same woman in the club? "You don't seem like you're only twenty-five. When I was twenty-five, I was still in my wild stage, but you have this wisdom, this intellectual beauty that I have never before encountered." He was impressed.

Semira laughed at him a little. She cleared her throat then replied. "That is because the brain does not fully develop until your late-twenties, so you were where you should have been developmentally. Besides, I can read people when I don't let my own opinions get in the way. I bet you weren't expecting me to say that, but I know passion when I see it. I know how it is to hunger and to reach and to get to the climax and to feel that rush, and then to challenge yourself more. That is how it is for me anyway," she shared as she lowered her eyes, feeling as if she had revealed too much of herself. Here she was, fully clothed, and felt as if she were naked before him. She needed to regain her composure and take control of her lips.

"Beautiful."

"What?" she asked as he took his hand and held hers.

"I said beautiful. You have a beautiful mind, a beautiful personality, and that makes you beautiful to me. So tell me, Beautiful, what are you passionate about?"

The flame from the candle caught his green eyes. She was quiet for a moment. He looked so lovely, his smooth skin felt like butter, and there was an urge within her to be close to him. She had no idea why her body was reacting the way it was. She caught his gaze, and she could mentally feel his lips connecting with hers. She pulled her hand away. It was shameful the way she was reaching. She couldn't believe herself. This was just how Natano had gotten her hooked.

Finally, their food came, and she was happy for the distraction. Inwardly, she was embarrassed by her schoolgirl behavior. Freshmen year was the last time she'd connected with anyone. She'd closed herself off after the heartbreak and betrayal. There was no need for love. Now, sitting across from this handsome man, she was feeling her defenses give way and that just could not happen. It would only end in heartbreak.

"Are you going to tell me what you are passionate about? Or, is that a question you are declining to answer?" he inquired, mystified by her.

"I think I have told you enough about me. Your life sounds a lot more interesting than mine." She felt a chill go through her. No one had ever asked her the questions he was asking. Not even Mariah.

"I don't know about that," he said. "So you have never had a boyfriend?"

She smirked at that question. "Samson forbade it, even though he was gone by the time I was of age. When my parents got divorced, my sister went wild and I just became more introverted and more into my books and studying. When I finally could date, I just didn't care to. I don't think I missed out on much. I mean…well never mind." She quickly hushed. He looked at her and she could tell he was pondering what was on her mind, but she didn't know him. There would always be Natano. It was not his business to know of him.

"What if I asked you out again?" She intrigued him. He wanted to know her better and spend more time understanding her. There was something so alluringly beautiful about her.

"I don't do hypothetical questions," she informed him, regaining her composure. She sat up and looked him straight in the eyes. He was indeed smooth, but she was not about to be swayed by fineness ever again. No one was going to break her heart or hurt her. She would not allow that to happen for the second time.

"Well, would you have dinner with me again?" he asked.

"I would be glad to," she replied as she ate her alfredo pasta.

He smiled at her. "So tell me something that no one knows about you?"

She looked at him and thought for a moment. "I don't think I have any secrets. I mean what you see, is what you get." She lied and asked for God's forgiveness. This was neither the time nor place to reveal her skeletons. She could not tell him what she had not told her family, the secret between her and Sophina.

"There is something," he challenged, as his eyes danced and a sly smile crept across his smooth face.

"My goodness, this is the first date," she replied, embarrassed by his directness.

"*Haha*, yeah it is. I just want to know everything I can about you. You are intriguing and unlike any other woman I have met. You are single?" he clarified.

"Yes, I'm very single. Are you?" she asked, staring into his eyes. She bet she was unlike any woman he had met because she was not falling into his lap. She had been raised on Christian values.

"Yeah, I told you I have been single a while," he reminded, wondering what she was hinting at.

4. Deonna

"I heard you, but being single has different meanings to different people. People say they are single but are dating three women at once, or having sex with a bunch of women. Maybe I should ask this question instead, are you dating anybody?" she asked.

"Yes, I am," he replied honestly.

Semira felt disgust rip across her face. "I knew it!" she snapped as she sipped her drink, becoming annoyed that she allowed herself to be taken by him. She knew better.

"If you knew it, why did you ask?" he asked, knowing he was getting under her skin. He thought she deserved it for how she had generalized all men last night at the restaurant. She needed to sweat just a little bit.

She sucked her teeth at his rude response. "Don't even try me because you will lose," she fumed, irritated. It was too good to be true. How in the world did she find herself in this situation? She'd just met him. What did she expect? She silently thought to herself. She was preparing to call a taxi to pick her up. She didn't need this and she certainly didn't need him.

"Would you like to know who she is?" he asked, sensing she was becoming more upset with him.

She decided to play along. "Sure, who is she?" Semira asked as she hit the send button to call a cab.

"You," he grinned with a wink.

She hit end on her cell phone and dropped it. Her mouth dropped wide open. "You are horrible, you know that? I was like two minutes from showing my tail and hurting your feelings. Don't do me that way." Now she felt idiotic and lowered her head in embarrassment of her recent thoughts.

"You should have seen your face. That was cute. I mean you were like, 'who is she?' I have got to tell my mom about that. Who were you calling?"

"Hush, you'll not tell her anything. You set me up," she fussed jokingly. "I was calling a cab."

He laughed more. "I wanted to know if you were interested," he said as he got up from the table to make sure she was okay.

"I'm fine. I'm a bit embarrassed, but I'm fine. I'll certainly get you back for that."

He smiled at her and offered her his hand. "Would you like to dance?"

In all the commotion, she had not realized that music was playing. "Sure, I can do a little two-step."

He walked her to the floor and pulled her close to his chest. His body towered over hers. She was glad she wore heels, making her taller. Without them, she was just five feet seven inches. He wrapped her body tight and pulled her close to his. She rested her head on his chest. His embrace was warm and tender. She closed her eyes and relished at the moment. He smelled sweet like vanilla bean and spice. She allowed herself to be free. "I like this," she confessed before she realized it.

"You like what?" he whispered, his lips turning up into a knowing smile.

She couldn't go back. She had opened the door. "I like feeling free." She was happy that Mariah pushed her. She needed it. She needed to face a fear. "I need some dessert now," she stated as she stepped back. She could feel herself wanting to be held longer and that was wrong. She needed to regain control and not allow herself to get lost. There was no reason to rush anything; they needed to take it slow, very slow. She would not get caught up in lustful emotions.

"Just one more dance and then we can have dessert," he told her and pulled her back to his chest. He knew conquering her would be a challenge, and he was sure she was close to breaking down at least one wall, if she would just stay in his arms.

Who was she to deny this man? She wanted one more dance too. As a matter of fact, she didn't want the night to end, but it had to. If she were not safe, she would end up hurt, bitter and a victim all over again. They danced one more song and then walked back to the table. The waiter brought their dessert and they enjoyed it. They talked a little more and then left the restaurant.

"Did you enjoy yourself?" he asked, kissing Semira's hand.

"I did. I had more fun than I thought I would," she admitted.

"I'm glad. We have another home game, and I would like for you to come."

She smiled. "Okay, I need to check my schedule. I will see what I can do."

"Good. Also, if you aren't busy Tuesday night, I would like to take you out to eat again."

"Well, going out during the week is difficult for me. How about I cook for you instead?" she offered. She didn't like leaving Nalani too much. There was not a man alive who could come between her and Nalani.

"I never turn down a home cooked meal. So still Tuesday?" he asked, smiling.

She shook her head. "Yes, still Tuesday. You can meet the love of my life," she said.

"Excuse me?" He looked at her funny.

Now who was getting in their feelings? "I mean my niece. Her name is Nalani. She's a sweet little girl."

He chuckled before replying, "Al lright then."

9. Deonna

She thought to herself that would be the true test. If Nalani liked him, then he had a chance, but if not, then he was out the door with no questions asked. It was just as important that she liked him, maybe even the most important. She would always choose her niece no matter what.

He smiled and they left the restaurant and headed back to her home. "My house is that one over there." He pulled up into the driveway and she thanked him once more for a wonderful evening. He got out and walked her to the door. She kissed his cheek and he tasted as sweet as he looked. He smiled and so did she.

"Goodnight, Carmine. I'll see you later."

"All right, beautiful," he intoned, admiring her radiant beauty and her home. She definitely had her own. He looked in awe at her spacious, lovely home. She lived in Oak Range, a nice area. She was definitely a boss. As he walked away, he noticed the Mercedes-Benz she had backed up. He thought he saw her leave the club in an Infiniti SUV, so she must have been big timing to be only in her mid-twenties. She was a catch and he was going to get her. There was something attractive about women who took care of their own and were not looking for a handout, but he hoped she was not so independent that she emasculated a man.

Once she was safe behind the door, Semira started leaping and screaming like a mad woman. She called Mariah, who was equally ecstatic and excited for Semira. She was so happy she didn't see her answering machine blinking. Once she did, she quickly hit play, assuming it was Nalani. Her mom had called and she wanted to know where Semira was. The next message was Nalani calling to tell Semira that she loved her, and then her sister. There was frantic in Sophina's voice and she wondered what trouble she had gotten into now. Semira hit delete and fell asleep. Whatever trouble she was in was going to have to wait until morning. Semira would put her back on the prayer list at church, but tonight was about her. She wanted to sleep without worry. No nightmares tonight, just sweet dreams.

Chapter 6

Monday morning started as usual, with Semira running around like a chicken with its head cut off making sure she and Nalani had all they needed. As long as she had been doing this, she thought her Mondays would go more smoothly, but they hadn't.

"Nalani, come on sweet pea, we have got to get moving. Now, do you have your lunch money?" Semira asked her, recalling last week she'd forgotten and Nalani had to borrow from Tobias. She'd felt like the worst parent for not remembering to ask her. Her mind sometimes broke off into a million pieces, allowing her to forget the most basic task.

"I'm taking my lunch today. Remember you made me a chicken salad sandwich, veggie sticks, yogurt and two Oreo cookies," Nalani said, smiling and placing her small hands in her Veggie Tales lunch box.

Semira hit herself in the head. "That is right, I almost forgot. I'm going to give you money anyway, just in case. What would I do without you, Lani?" she asked, kissing her forehead.

Nalani looked at her and gave her a big toothless smile. Semira kissed her cheek, grabbed her hand, and they walked out of the door. Semira buckled her in her seatbelt and they were off. They started singing Jimmy Needham as loud as they could. Semira loved his smooth, unique voice, and his music was her testimony.

"I hope you have a wonderful day at school. Remember you are riding the church van and I will pick you up a little after five o'clock. I love you!!" Semira said, hugging her once more.

"I love you too. I'll see you at five, Aunt Se Se."

Semira watched her walk into the school. She was growing up so fast, too fast it seemed. It seemed like just yesterday her sister had her. She recalled her delivery. They'd hid her pregnancy until Sophina had delivered. Semira stood by her side even though she'd gotten pregnant by the man she loved. That had been the most traumatic time of her life. Nalani hadn't been the healthiest baby in the world, but with time, she grew stronger. Semira was glad. She prayed to God constantly to just heal her and He did. Now she was a little firecracker. Semira loved it.

Once she arrived at work, there were several messages awaiting her. Many of them were from Sophina. The sound of her voice made Semira slump in her seat. She worried for her and she prayed for her, now she wondered what she would have to do for her. Semira debated for a moment, slowly picked up the phone, and dialed the number Sophina left. She heard a soft voice on the other end. Sophina talked and Semira listened. Her voice sounded weak, her tone sad. It took Semira back to when she'd started using drugs. Finally, she said to her what she had said to Seth. Sophina wanted money. Semira shook her head. It was always money. "I'm not sending you money in Las Vegas for you to blow it. If you come home, I will do all I can to help you, but I'm not supporting Dante or your drug habit," Semira fussed sternly.

Sophina was silent. The longer she was silent, the angrier Semira got. "Sophina, don't you want to know about Nalani and how she is? I mean, she hasn't heard from you in months and hasn't seen you in a year, almost two years."

4. Deonna

"She is with you and I know she is safe. Look, I really need that money. Just send me two hundred and forty dollars, and then I can get back on my feet," she implored, fiending for a hit.

"Sophina, I don't feel right about it. Why won't you come home? Is Dante hurting you? We can send you a ticket. I'm not helping you help Dante." Semira was so fed up with her attraction to this man who she was so infatuated with. She would lose her life behind some no good, two timing idiot. Although she'd taken Natano from her, he was the best guy she ever had and she wished she had stayed with him. At least then, she would know that she was well provided for, but Dante was a nut and thug wannabe. She could not stand him. Sophina loved that sort of man. It was beyond Semira's comprehension.

She took a deep breath before replying, "Stop being like that. Dante loves me. Are you going to help me?"

Semira didn't want to, but who else would help her if she didn't? She was far better to Sophina than she ever was to Semira. "Look this is the last time so don't call me again asking for money. I'm going to send you the money, but this is it," she reiterated. "If you spend it on drugs or give it to that pig, then that is on you. I will not help you anymore. You need to get your life together. I'm going to send it Western Union," Semira told her, even though she hated doing it. She knew it was wrong, but unlike Seth, she had a hard time rejecting her. She could talk a good talk but when it came to her sister, she was more like her mother than her brother. She only wished Sophina were like that to her.

"Thank you, Semira. I know I can always count on you. Will you tell Nalani I love her?"

"I will." Semira hung up the phone. She was so frustrated with her. Once lunchtime rolled around, she went to the Western Union. She couldn't believe she was doing this again. Semira had said the last time was it, but here she was again, bailing Sophina out again. She had to stop. Semira got back in the car and her cell rang. "Hello," she said, using her professional voice.

"Hey there, beautiful. I wanted to know if you had time to meet me for lunch," Carmine requested.

Her heart started pounding from dealing with her sister. It was kind of him to ask her to go out to lunch, but now was not a good time. There were other things she had to tend to. "I wish I could, but I only have thirty minutes and I'm heading to a drive-thru."

"I understand. I will call you later tonight."

"Okay. Thanks for calling. You just made a bad day better."

4. Deonna

He heard the worry in her voice. "What's the matter?" His voice sounded concerned.

"My sister. You know, it is one of those stories to tell when you have time. I shouldn't have even brought it up. I will call you tonight, and I hope you have a great day."

"Thanks and you too. I mean, cheer up. If you need to talk, just call me," he offered.

"Thank you. Bye." They hung up and she went to the drive-thru to get her food. The rest of the day seemed to just go. Her mother called her with some interesting information. It seemed that Sophina had gotten two hundred dollars from her too, which infuriated Semira that she'd lied. It was her fault for breaking the rules, but never again. Sophina had not changed, but Semira was going to. She finished her work, said goodbye to her co-workers, and headed to the church. Nalani was outside playing. She walked behind her and picked her up.

"Hey there, sweet pea. How was your day?" Semira questioned, looking her over to make sure she didn't have any bruises. Some might consider her a bit overprotective. She cared about her niece as well as her nephew. They were not going to live the life she'd lived. Growing up the way she had made her more cautious than most people.

"Auntie Se Se, I'm so glad to see you. I had a great day. I got all good grades on my report card," Nalani gushed, proud of herself.

"You did? Well, that means we have to celebrate. I'm so proud of you. Go get your bags and we can go home." She took off like a bullet. Semira wanted her to always be that happy. She didn't care what her momma said; she was going to adopt her. She had to keep Nalani safe. She came running down the steps with her book bag and lunch bag and got into the car. As Semira pulled away from the church, Semira asked Nalani if she would like to go out to dinner to celebrate her accomplishment. Nalani nodded her head in agreement.

"Auntie, my class is having a mother-daughter tea and I wanted to know if you could come."

"Honey, of course, I'll be there. I would love to have tea with you," Semira praised, winking at her.

She looked down at her hands and then back at her Auntie Se Se. There was something on her mind. Semira could tell by the way her brow was lifted. "Sweet pea, what's the matter?"

"I was just wondering," her words long were and drawn out.

4. Deonna

"Wondering about what?" Semira asked her as she took her hand and held her face. "Tell me what's going on in that little head of yours."

"You take me everywhere, and you come to all my activities. Why can't you be my momma?" Her little innocent eyes stared at Semira's.

"Your momma is great too. She called me today and told me how much she loved you," Semira shared, fudging the truth, but she was sure that if Sophina was not drugged up, that would be the truth.

"I know. You tell me that all the time, but she never comes to see me. I don't even remember her anymore," she confessed.

"Now Lani, don't be that way. She loves you and she wants what's best for you. You know how special you are. You have so many people who love and care for you. You have your grandparents, me, Uncle Seth, Auntie Beth, Uncle Blaine and Auntie Riah," Semira reminded her, smiling. She wanted to change the mood to make her feel a little better. "Guess what? I have some news too," Semira added as she tickled her rosy red cheeks.

"Tell me, tell me," she implored, her little curls bouncing as she jumped up and down. The older she got, the more she looked like Natano. It made Semira wonder if the rest of her friends noticed how much Nalani looked like her daddy.

"Well, I have met a friend and he is coming for dinner tomorrow."

"Really, who is he?" she asked excitedly.

Sometimes she swore Nalani was far older than her age. "His name is Carmine."

Her face lit up. "You mean Carmine Pontiero? Oh my, he is a great point guard. He's cute. You know they traded him from Miami to here. He wasn't performing very well, but he is doing better now."

Semira sat back, shocked. She had no idea she liked basketball like that. "How did you know that?"

"Uncle Seth has been teaching me. So Carmine is coming to our house? I can't wait. Do you think he will autograph my basketball?"

"I think we can manage that." Semira was surprised by her reaction. They finished dinner and headed home. Semira gave her a bath and prepared her for bed.

"Can I stay up until nine tonight?" she asked with that sparkle in her eyes that would make Semira give in to her, no matter what she asked.

"Since you made the Principal's honor roll, I think that can be arranged," Semira told her and kissed the tip of her nose.

4. Deonna

"Thank you." She ran, jumped on Semira, and gave her a big wet kiss on the side of her face. They lay on the couch and watched Uptv until it was her bedtime. Nalani read a story to Semira and after they said Nalani's prayers, Semira tucked her in.

She sat there for a while and watched her fall asleep. She wanted to protect her, and it hurt her heart that she was in so much pain. No child should have to feel like their mother didn't care. She would never understand Sophina. Knowing how their dad treated them, she thought she would have been a better mother. She had the most incredible little girl and she chose a man and drugs over her own flesh and blood. It was the worst kind of betrayal. Semira kissed Nalani one more time, and then went downstairs and dialed Carmine.

He picked up on the third ring. "How are you doing?" she asked as she made herself comfortable on the couch.

"I'm good. How are you? You sounded distracted this afternoon."

As she leaned back, she took a deep breath. The house grew silent as if it knew what she wanted to say. "My sister is just making things difficult," Semira managed to say. It was difficult for her to share that tiny bit of information because it made her feel weak. She was supposed to be able to handle anything that was thrown her way.

"I hope I'm not digging too much, but how is it that you have your sister's daughter?" he asked curiously.

"Mm..., well my sister got into drugs. She got pregnant with Nalani during my freshman year of college, but during that time she was doing drugs, drinking, and partying like a nut. She used to come see her, now she just calls me for money. So today was one of those days. She lied to me. It is tough sometimes." She could feel a migraine coming on. It was a shame how her sister could still have that type of effect on her. Semira promised herself she wouldn't allow Sophina to treat her that way, but she still allowed it. First, it was Samson and now her sister. She wished she didn't care so much. She wished she could erase all of the hurt, but no matter how busy she kept her schedule, it seemed to always find her. So much was stolen from her and so much was expected of her. She felt so lonely.

It was hard at times being her and having unhealed wounds bleed at will. Sometimes she felt like she didn't have a right to be angry. In feeling compelled to always do the right thing, she suffered because she didn't want to see another suffer, but she suffered in silence. Weeping in the night and smiling in the morning, if her insides had been outside, the world would know her secrets. She wondered if her sister felt the same way about her. Did she even want to be a family again? Semira wanted to love her and have her back, but she

4. Deonna

knew that Sophina was incapable of caring or loving anyone other than herself, Dante, and drugs.

"You were like nineteen taking care of your sister's baby and going to school?" Carmine asked, both impressed and astonished. No wonder she was so controlled.

"I was seventeen, and I was working at the bank to feed us. My mom didn't know she had a child. We hid the heck out of the pregnancy. I was supposed to keep the secret, but then it got hard, and my mom found out after a year. She was so angry with me, but I thought I was protecting everyone. I would not have it any other way," she shared, smiling just thinking about Nalani. She was worth every adversity and sacrifice Semira ever made.

"You are a great sister," he stated.

"Not really. I just do what I have to for my baby girl. You know that she is so excited about you coming over. She told me your whole background and on the way home, she told me your stats. I didn't even know she liked basketball," Semira said to him.

"She is a fan? It sounds to me like she has taste," he boasted.

Semira laughed out loud. "Yeah, she wants your autograph."

"You tell her I would be honored," he replied.

Then he was silent for a moment as if he were thinking about something.

"So tell me what you are passionate about?"

His question took her aback. She thought it was odd that he wanted to know so badly. "Where did that come from?" she asked. Why would he even care?

She pretended to be so stone cold. He saw right through her. "You never told me. I want to know."

"I care about people, especially children," she shared.

"Wow, you have a big heart. I would have never known that if I hadn't taken you out. So where is your sister?"

She didn't like talking about her that much, but she guessed if she wanted to have a decent relationship, she was going to have to open up a little. "I think she is in Las Vegas with her boyfriend. Seeing her is another reason why I shy from relationships. She can always find the worst scum," Semira confided, not meaning to show her real feelings. Sophina was wasting her beauty and talent on men unworthy of her. She seemed not to understand her worth and value. That was surprising to Semira because Sophina had been so popular and pretty before she allowed drugs to overtake her life.

He wondered what pain and heartbreak she'd had in her life. "You were ice cold to me because of your family's past. I wish people knew how their treatment of others affected that individual's life. I'm not that kind of man. I'm just a man who is determined to make you mine. I don't care how long it takes to convince you because you are well worth the time."

Semira could feel the excitement inside of her body, but she was also aware that a man would say anything to get what he wanted. What did she really know about Carmine? Then there was the part of her she thought she had shut off and completely detached herself from. That part of her that wanted to be seen, to have someone just care about her and for her. "You know how to flatter a lady. I'm not judging you. I know you aren't my father or a deadbeat. I just have a jaded view or should I say I had a jaded view," she asserted as she turned off the television so she could hear him better.

"So how about we make a deal," he offered.

She thought for a moment. She had a tendency to get in her own head and create situations that hadn't occurred. Now she was trying to do better. She was still hesitant. "It depends on the terms of that deal," she replied.

"Well, you won't make any judgments about me based on the actions of others, and I will do the same."

"That sounds fine to me. I can handle that. Oh, I almost forgot. Do you want any specific meal tomorrow or do you want me to surprise you?"

"You can surprise me. I just like good cooking. I don't care what it is as long as it tastes great," he confessed, missing his father's homemade pasta dishes.

"Okay, I can do that. It's getting late and I have to get up early. I will see you tomorrow."

"You sure will. What time?" he asked.

"How about six-thirty p.m.? Or, is that too late?"

"No, that is perfect. That gives me enough time to shower after practice. You have a restful night, and don't let people take away the joy that God gives."

Once he said that, she felt a tingle go up her spine. He had a way of saying things and she liked that about him. She liked that he wasn't bashful, and she liked his calming attitude. She was becoming smitten with him. "Thank you for listening and hearing me. You have a good night as well, and we'll see you tomorrow. Sweet dreams." They hung up and Semira found herself acting like a teenager. She went running to her room to write in her diary. That man had hit a note. She was ready to sing.

~~~

Semira and Nalani went through their routine. Nalani was in a good mood. She kept talking about Carmine and she suggested they have chicken fettuccini as a main course meal, and that Semira should make monkey bread for dessert, and her

4. Deonna

famous spinach shrimp almond salad. Semira couldn't believe she was having that conversation with a seven-year-old. Nalani was very advanced for her age.

Once they arrived at school, Nalani gave her a big hug and kiss, and then placed three fingers upon her heart and rotated them around her heart which meant, "I love you with all my heart." She watched her walk into the school and then she went to work.

Semira's workday went smoothly. After work, she went to pick up Nalani and they went to the grocery store and picked up the things they needed and headed home. She had an hour to get cute and cook. She started working. At six o'clock, she changed clothes and started making her salad while the food was simmering. She put the monkey bread in the oven. Nalani came running down the steps. "It smells so good in here. Do you need me to help?" Her sweet voice penetrated through the kitchen.

Semira smiled at hearing her. "Yes, ma'am, I do. I need you to set the table." She was glad to do it. While she set the table, Semira put the finishing touches on the salad. Then the doorbell rang. Nalani ran ahead of her to answer it. Carmine stood there with two sets of flowers in his hand. He gave one to Semira and one to Nalani. Nalani loved it. She grabbed his hand and walked him into the family room and started to talk. Semira excused herself and set the food on the table. "All right you two, it is time to eat." They walked hand in hand to the table. They sat down and Semira said grace.

"Semira, do I smell chicken fettuccini?" Carmine asked her.

"Yeah, you can thank Nalani for that. She decided tonight's meal," Semira replied.

He looked at her and smiled. "You know, Nalani, chicken fettuccini is my favorite. Did you help cook it?"

"No, but I set the table," she said, showing her toothless grin. She was proud to let it be known that she had done so.

He winked at her and she winked back and then smiled at Semira. She excused herself again and brought out the salad and main meal course meal. They jumped into it. Carmine seemed to enjoy himself. He patted his stomach as if to say he was full.

"Carmine, you have to save some room for dessert, and believe me, it is good stuff," Semira bragged.

"You ladies have outdone yourselves. This is really good. So what kind of dessert do you have?"

"I made monkey bread."

He looked at her as if to say *what?*

"Just wait until you taste it, you will love it." Semira went to get it and brought it out with ice cream, because Nalani loved chocolate ice cream. She watched Carmine take a bite and she could tell by his face that he liked it. Nalani got out of her seat and sat on Semira's lap and began to eat her dessert. They talked a little and then Nalani excused herself. Five minutes later, she reappeared with a Sharpie and her basketball for Carmine to sign. Semira burst out laughing.

"What's so funny?" she asked her, looking confused.

"Nothing, sweet pea. I just didn't think you really wanted his autograph."

"The kids didn't believe me when I told them he was coming, but now I have proof. Can I come to your game this week?" she asked as she changed her direction from Semira to Carmine.

"Well, if Semira says that you can. I will even introduce you to the team," he offered as he winked at her and then smiled at Semira.

"Of course, you can go to the game. I'm sure we will have a ball." Her little face lit up and she went prancing and dancing around the room.

Semira started to clean up the table and put up the leftovers. Carmine also helped her.

"Your niece is a spit fire. You certainly have done a wonderful job raising her. She has quite the personality. She is a lot friendlier than you are," he teased through chuckles.

She looked at him and sucked her teeth. How was he throwing shade at her in her own home? "Whatever! She is my heart. That little lady is the best part of me. I love her more and more every day," she gushed as she dried the last dish and turned away from him.

Instantly, she felt the gentle breeze of his breath kiss the side of her neck, and he took his hand and caressed her hair. For a moment, she was breathless and baffled not knowing how to react, and then she closed her eyes, ready to feel his embrace. She waited, but it never came. She turned around and his olive eyes met hers. Her mind was screaming all kinds of things to do, but she rejected each, not having the boldness to make the first move. "Excuse me," she breathlessly said as she walked around him, breaking the awkward tension between them. "I need to check on Nalani. She is a bit too quiet." Semira walked out of the kitchen and found Nalani watching her favorite video, *Angel Wings*. "Lani, do you need anything?" She sat down and pretended to tickle her.

"No, Auntie, I'm good. Where is Carmine?" she asked through giggles.

"Here I am." His voice made Semira jump. She didn't know he had walked into the family room.

4. Deonna

Nalani turned toward him. "In a little while, I have to put on my night clothes and go to bed. Will you read me a story?"

He looked at Semira and she nodded. "I would love to," he replied with a smile.

"*Yes!*" She was as happy as could be. Semira took her to the bathroom and washed her up, then she ran to get Carmine so he could read her a story. They took turns reading and Semira tucked her in and kissed her goodnight.

"Thank you, Carmine. You certainly didn't have to do that, but I appreciate you taking the time with her. She will remember that forever," Semira told him.

Nalani's reaction to him made Semira recall what Mariah said. She needed a male role model in her life. Maybe it was time for Semira to open her heart again. Maybe she was afraid for no reason at all. Didn't God say fear not? It seemed that Semira feared love and she didn't want to be that way. She wanted to be fearless, not afraid and not bitter.

"I should be thanking you. I like Nalani," he shared.

Semira thought to herself *how you could not*. Nalani was just the greatest child of all. "Did you enjoy yourself?" she asked as they sat down in front of the television. He was so handsome, and she found him engaging, especially how he'd handled her niece.

He scooted closer to Semira. "I had a great time. This was much better than I had planned. You sure can cook. I haven't had a meal that good since I left my momma's house. So thank you for that." He smiled and put his arm around Semira's shoulders. She leaned into him, just wanting to fall asleep in his arms.

"I feel like we have some unfinished business to attend to," he stated without hesitation.

She glanced up at him strangely. She had no idea what he was talking about. "What?"

His eyes caught hers, he pulled her closer, and his lips grazed hers as if he was testing the waters. Then she felt his lips tarry on hers and he moved them in such a way that paralyzed her. It was good Natano had taught her how to kiss because this could've been awkward. Still, in her mind, she was praying to God not to make a fool of herself. He had touched her like only one man had in a long time. She didn't want the kiss to end. She wanted it to last until she was out of breath.

The phone started to ring. At first, she was mad, and then she thought it was God's intervention. She pulled away and picked up the phone. "Hello?" she asked in a low agitated voice. "Who is this?"

"It's Sophina. Look, I want to come home. I want to see Nalani and y'all."

4. Deonna

"Okay, fine. Just come home." Semira was hoping she would get the hint that she was calling at a bad time, but it wasn't sinking in.

"I need you to send me some more money. So I can fly home," she explained.

Semira had forgotten she had a guest in the house and her voice grew loud with irritation. "I just sent you two hundred and forty dollars and mom sent you two hundred. That is enough to fly on a cheaper airline and if not, you better call Greyhound because I refuse to give you more money. What I have is for me and Nalani. I can't keep you up and us too," she snapped, angrily that she was starting this again. She was a user. She used drugs and she used people. Right now, Semira was tired of being used.

"Now, don't be that way. Why are you being so mean and spiteful? You know if you needed it and I had it, I would give it to you. We are sisters we have to look out for each other," Sophina whined.

Semira knew that was a lie when it left her lips. Her sister liked to manipulate, but she was not falling for it this time. "I needed you, but as I remember you weren't there. Don't play that game with me. Besides, if you really want to come home you will, but don't you bring Dante here. Where is he? He took you out there, he can't bring you home?" she fussed. She could hear him in the background sounding like a baboon. He made her sick. Semira had a good mind to take a belt and beat him. That was his problem; no one ever punished him. Everyone feared him, but not her.

"Fine, be that way. I don't care." Then she hung up hard, making Semira's ears ring.

She was too old for this and so was Semira. She slumped into the chair. She hated this emotional stress she allowed Sophina to cause, but she was her sister. Sophina was older than she was. She should be looking out for Semira, not Semira supporting her. Sophina had to learn that she was not going to do it anymore. She no longer had the energy or mental ability to handle the drama of Sophina.

"Semira, are you okay? Who was on the phone?" Carmine asked her as he walked over. His touch was warm. She just wanted to lie on his shoulder and forget everything.

"My sister called me. She wants more money. She said she was coming home. I don't know. I just can't keep doing this," she stressed, running her fingers through her long hair. "She will probably call Momma, who will break her back giving her the money, then come here for a week or two, play momma and disrupt Nalani, and I will have to pick up the pieces. I'm tired. I'm so tired of being used," she confessed. She could feel her pulse rate increase and her body shake.

4. Deonna

"Come here. Just let me hold you," he offered.

She needed to be held. She had not known that before, but being in his arms made her wonder how she had gone so long without it. It made her remember Natano. She closed her eyes and hoped Carmine was the one God had put on this earth for her.

Carmine kissed her forehead and held her tightly. He spoke encouraging words and he listened to her. He didn't just listen, he heard her. At midnight, she woke up, still in his arms. He looked so peaceful sleeping. She didn't want to wake him. She tried to maneuver so she wouldn't disturb his sleep, but as soon as she got up his eyes slowly opened.

"I'm sorry," she whispered in his ear. "I didn't mean to wake you up."

"That is fine. What time is it?"

"It's midnight. I guess you better get ready to go."

He slowly rose and stretched his arms. She could see the outline of his body and she couldn't help but smile. "Here, let me give you a plate. I figured since you like it so much, you might want to take some home."

He yawned and tried to speak at the same time. She presumed that meant yes. She got his plate and he started to gather his belongings. "Beautiful, you keep your head up. I'm sure your sister will get her act together, but you know you're only responsible for you and Nalani, not your sister. Let me see you smile," he prompted.

She could feel herself melting. Finally, someone was in her corner. She smiled and he leaned down to kiss her. She walked him to the door and watched him get into his SUV and drive off. He was right; at times, she was as worse as her mother. There was a part of her that hoped Sophina would get her act together. She wasn't Semira's responsibility, and she couldn't let her stress her anymore. She went to check on Nalani. She was sound asleep. Semira prayed to God that she wasn't suffering, and that she knew how much she was loved. One thing was for sure, Semira would give her life for Nalani's safety and happiness. She kissed her once more, then walked softly back to her bedroom and fell asleep instantly, dreaming of love.

7. Deonna

Chapter 7

"Mom, you should come with us to the game. I want you to meet Carmine. We have talked every night on the phone and Nalani is crazy about him. I bet you would like him," Semira suggested to her mother as she was putting Nalani in her seatbelt. Mariah was helping Tobias. "The tickets are free. You sure you don't want to go?"

"I'm sure. I'm going to see if Sophina shows up. Just invite him over for Sunday dinner. Then he can meet the whole family," she said, excited her daughter finally found a man.

However, Semira was disappointed in her reply. The one time she wanted her support, her mother felt that Sophina needed it more and they both knew Sophina probably wouldn't show up anyway. "Fine, Mom, just tell Seth to pick Tobias up at my house, or if he wants he can let him spend the night," she replied, openly annoyed and irritated.

"Okay, baby, I will tell him. You all have a fun time." Her mom smiled and waved goodbye, unaware of Semira's dismay.

Semira got into her car and drove to the auditorium. She could feel Mariah's eyes on her, but Semira didn't want to talk about it. It didn't matter anyway. This was about the kids having fun. She knew her mother and this was no surprise. There was no reason to feel bitter because this was her reality. It was her fault for having expectations. The kids' eyes were full of bewilderment. It was the first time they had gone to a live basketball game. Semira had taken them to football games but never a basketball game. She was happy just watching them. They walked inside and she went to meet Carmine, and as promised, he took the kids to meet the players. Mariah nudged Semira to follow because she wanted to meet the team too. So they went as well. The guys were really nice to Tobias and Nalani, signing their shirts and answering their questions. Carmine walked up to Semira and gave her a warm hug.

"I got a feeling you all are going to win."

"You do? In that case, I better play hard," he joked playfully.

"I better get these kids before they run you all mad. Thank you for letting them meet the players. I will see you on the floor. Play hard." She grinned and went to get Tobias and Nalani. You would have thought they had gone to Disney World the way they were acting. They walked to the stands, and their jaws jabbed the entire time. They grew silent when the game started and cheered for Carmine like they had known him forever. He played well, in fact, the whole team did, and they won the game. Semira winked at Mariah and she winked back.

"You really like him, don't you?" Mariah commented with a grin.

4. Deonna

Semira looked at her. "Girl, he's cool. It's not like I'm falling in love. I would like to get to know him better. Nalani likes him a lot. We'll see how things go. I like to go slow," she told her as the crowd started to thin out.

"It will all work out. He is the only man who has made you sparkle since your infatuation with Natano. I could tell at the club he had something and you were ready to dismiss that man," she replied, playfully pinching her.

"I know, you are right. But it is looking really good right now. I'm not going to get my hopes up too high," Semira explained, purposely avoiding the topic of Natano.

"You like him a lot. You are shining like a star, girl," Mariah teased. Semira hadn't looked like that since Natano. She really loved that boy. She didn't think Mariah was aware but she knew. It was sad to see how heartbroken she was when he went away. At least, Carmine was bringing her spark back.

Semira put her hands over her face. She felt like a kid with a crush. Mariah was right. In the two weeks she'd spent with Carmine, she was different. It was different in a good way. He was definitely an asset to her personality.

A while later, the kids were ready to go. So Mariah walked them to the car and Semira waited on Carmine. She congratulated him on his win. He was excited and asked her to join him and the team as they celebrate the victory.

"I would love to, but I have two kids staying with me tonight. Can I get a rain check?" she asked, wishing she could spend time with him.

"I almost forgot about Nalani and Tobias. I guess I will have to accept a rain check," he pouted disappointedly.

"Oh, if you have time, my mom has invited you to Sunday dinner, but you know if you have something else to do, then don't worry about it."

"I will be there. You just tell me the time and place. In fact, I'll go to church with you."

Semira smiled. "Okay, well I won't keep you long. I know you want to celebrate, so go have a good time, and call me when you get in, just so I know you got home safe." She tugged on his jersey.

"I wish you could come. If you can stop by, we are partying at the Blue Lagoon."

She nodded her head and kissed him with a passion she knew would make him miss her. When she pulled back, he was still recovering. That was how she liked to leave them, wanting more.

"Wait a minute you can't kiss me like that and walk away," he told her as he reached out to pull her back.

"Yes I can. Now you have to get ready to go out. I will call you. Bye." She waved goodbye and pulled out of his hold.

4. Deonna

He was cutting up, saying she was breaking his heart. If he thought that was heartbreaking, he hadn't seen anything yet. When she got to the car, the kids had fallen asleep.

"Mariah, they are having a party and there is a part of me that wants to go, but what am I going to do with the kids?"

"Let your brother keep them or even me," she offered with a smile.

"I can't go there without you," Semira told her. She didn't even like clubs, and she sure was not going without her best friend.

"Okay, call Seth and ask him."

Semira dialed his number and he said he would which was surprising to her. So she took them to his house and kissed them and tucked them into bed. Seth and Marybeth were happy to have them. He wanted Semira to go out. That was why she loved Seth—his heart was so big. She loved Marybeth because she loved her brother. She was good to him and their entire family.

Mariah and Semira arrived at Semira's house to change clothes and then they drove to the Blue Lagoon. The party had been going for an hour so they were making an entrance. She walked to the front of the line, told the cat at the door who she was, and he let them in. She was cold but cute. She had her legs and her arms out. When they walked in, the music was bumping, and guys were grabbing their hands trying to spit game. That was why she hated to come into clubs, because it was like men and some women too, forgot their manners. If her mother knew, she'd have a fit. Good girl Semira wasn't about the club life but she wanted Carmine. She spotted him. It wasn't hard; just look for all the guys over six -five feet tall. He was standing on the dance floor with some of the players and some females. "Mariah, follow me and watch this." Semira walked to the middle of the dance floor directly in his path of sight and performed like she was Beyoncé. The crowd backed up because when Mariah and Semira danced, they commanded the floor. It was on.

Carmine thought his eyes were playing tricks on him because it looked like Semira was on the dance floor, but he was sure she wasn't coming. Plus, she wasn't a fan of clubbing. He tapped his friend Leon, and said, "I think that's my girl dancing out there."

"Yes, that's her and her friend Mariah," Leon confirmed. They were both looking fine.

Carmine nodded in agreement. That was Semira. "I didn't know she had those kinds of moves. Church girls!" he teased, running out to the floor to get a closer look. "Beautiful, what are you doing here?" he asked as he wrapped his arms around her neck.

4. Deonna

"I decided I wanted to come and celebrate too," she told him smiling.

"Hold on, let me see you." He turned her around and pulled her close. "You are leaving me speechless right now. I saw you walk to the floor and I was like is that my girl. Nah, I must be seeing things, and Leon was like that looks like Semira and Mariah, and I saw you dancing I was like, what. You're looking good!!

"I'm glad you came. You're so fine in that outfit. Come over here. I want to introduce you."

Semira grabbed Mariah, they walked upstairs to VIP, and he introduced them to the players again. They were nice, and Mariah decided she wanted to flirt with as many as she could but Leon was trying hard to get her attention.

"Where are Nalani and Tobias?" Carmine asked her and they sat down on the velvet couch. She had never been into the Blue Lagoon, but it was nice. There were huge fish tanks with exotic fish and the whole place looked like paradise. "Semira, did you hear me?"

"Sorry, I was just looking at this place. It's spectacular. But to answer your question, they are staying with my brother and sister-in-law. He was glad to have them," she answered and she crossed her legs and rested her head on the couch.

"Wow, you know you are making it hard for me to concentrate," he confessed. He just didn't know what to expect from her. When he thought he knew her, she pulled another twist.

"How so?" she acted as if she didn't know. She knew she looked good. She was not about to lose another guy because she was seen as stiff and controlled. She could let loose, be attractive, and still a Christian.

He smiled at her. "I just love how you rocking that outfit. You've been holding out on me."

She just smiled and acted as if she wasn't fazed. He pulled her closer to him and she rested her body against his. As she arranged herself to get comfortable, one of his friends stopped by and started to talk to him. "Yo, C this you?" he asked, nodding toward Semira.

Semira started laughing. He was talking about her as if she was not sitting there.

"Yeah, Rey, this my lady, Semira." Carmine boasted, looking at him.

She didn't know she was his lady, but he had said it enough throughout the night. She found that she was okay with that.

4. Deonna

"It's nice to meet you, Rey," Semira said to him as she extended her hand. His grip was strong, but gentle at the same time.

He smiled at her. "It is a pleasure to meet you as well, sweetheart. I don't know how C got him a bad chick like you, but if he slips up, come holla at ya boy!" he replied and kissed her hand.

"All right, Rey, you're doing the most. If you used that kind of skill on the court, we might make it to the finals. Now back off my lady, she unavailable," he told him and straight mean muged.

Rey grinned and winked at Semira before leaving.

Semira could not contain herself. She erupted with laughter. Carmine was so cute. She nudged him and he laughed too. "You're so funny. That was cute, but you can't give him a hard time. The man has taste. He knows when he sees fine things," she commented flirtatiously. It was not even like her to be that way. She liked it.

"You know you're a bad girl. I like that in you though." He winked at her and they enjoyed the night.

~~~

Another sunny day in the desert, Sophina thought to herself. She caught a glimpse of her face in the mirror, and she was frightened by what she saw. She wasn't the beauty queen she had been in high school; she looked tired and old. Her face still held a touch of youth, somewhere packed deep inside. Hidden behind drugs, self-violation, and beatings, there was a good person in her. She wanted to be good, but she had been bad for so long she had lost her way. Her sister had been good to her even though she had violated her sister in the worse way not once but numerous times. She looked out the window again and wondered how she had become the woman she now was.

"Sophina, what yam doin' lookin' out there like ya want to run away or something? Come back in here and let me love you." The loud boom of Dante's voice brought her back to reality. She heard Dante's voice, but she thought if she ignored him for a while he would let her be, let her have some peace.

"Woman don't ya hear me talking to ya? Get in here!" Like an obedient child, she walked to him and together they snorted the last of the cocaine. "Now we can go back to North Carolina and hit up your sister for some cash. Is she goin' to send us the money?"

"No, she ain't. She told me to take the bus."

"Ain't she a selfish heffa? That's just like her high-class know-it-all walk on water self. She thinks she better than us anyway. You 'bout as worthless as yo sista. Well, come on and get ya stuff packed up. You's bout to work all night to get the money we need."

4. Deonna

"Aiight, Dante." Sophina sobbed as her mind slowly drifted to another place. She liked feeling like she could fly, like she was invincible. She leaned her head on Dante and went to sleep.

"Babe, get up. We gotta start the ride back home." Dante shook her aggressively to wake her up.

She had burnt out. She slowly came to. "Dante," she whined as if she were a baby. "I don't want to get up right now. Let me have five more minutes."

"No, we gotta get goin' now so come on. Get ya stuff or I'll leave you."

She rolled out of bed, brushed her teeth, and followed Dante out the door. She was furious with Semira for not sending her a plane ticket. That was the least she could do for her older sister. Instead of staying in that moment, she removed the thought out of her mind and got on the bus. It would be a long ride—a very long ride. She hoped she would be able to get through without having to take a hit. As she and Dante got on the bus, eyes stared at them. She instantly felt ashamed of what she had on. Her jeans were full of holes and her shirt was ripped. She hadn't thought to make herself look nice. She untied her long black hair and let it hang in her face. She leaned close to Dante, closed her eyes, and began to rest. She started to daydream. How had she become this?

Chapter 8

The entire family was in the kitchen. They were talking about Carmine, and from what Semira heard, they liked him. She smiled at herself. He was a great catch. She asked Nalani to set the table and to wash her hands. She did, and then she turned to Semira with a smile and asked," Auntie Se Se, can I sit beside Carmine?"

"Yes, ma'am you can. You really like him, don't you?" Semira surmised.

She smiled at her and put up her thumb. "I hope he's a keeper." She winked at her and ran to the kitchen.

Semira laughed to herself. She knew Nalani had been around grown folks too long, mostly her G-Momma.

"Come on you all, it is time to eat," Semira called out. As soon as the words left her mouth, she heard the feet pounding on the floor. It sounded like a herd of buffalo. That made her smile. For a moment, it was like old times. The whole family except for Sophina was there. They all sat down, said grace, and began to pass the food around. The table was full of laughter and conversation. Carmine fit well with the family and Semira enjoyed that. Seth had even taken to him. Semira's mom smiled and winked. She was just glad there was a man in her life. Right as Semira was biting into her turkey, her mom started to tell one of her embarrassing stories.

4. Deonna

"Momma, come on now. Can we not tell that one again?" Semira implored. It was not necessary.

Her mother nodded. "Carmine, you just remind me and I will tell you when she isn't around."

Semira rolled her eyes and continued eating. Then the doorbell rang. She looked strangely at her momma and she looked back at Semira. Momma got up and answered the door. Everyone continued to talk and eat, so Semira did the same. Two minutes later, Ella appeared with a smile and Sophina. Semira gasped. Sophina looked like a hurricane had run over her. She ran right to Nalani and hugged her, but Nalani pushed away. Semira got up and saw Dante hanging in the family room. He had some nerve. His clothes were sagging and oversized. His eyes were bloodshot red. He looked like the devil. The room grew silent. Carmine looked lost. She felt a rage of anger as she saw the reason her sister had left her only child.

"Look y'all, it's Sophina. She has come home," Ella said, clasping her hands like it was the best news ever. Then she quickly prepared a place for Soph to sit.

Nalani got up and ran to sit with Semira. She looked scared of her mother. Instantly, Semira became protective of her. She loved her sister, but she didn't trust her. She wasn't trustworthy. She'd give her sister almost anything, but she would not give her Nalani. The attorney working for her was nearly finished with the adoption papers and they were going to court in two weeks to make it final. She wished she had done it earlier, but she was now financially stable and there was no reason she could not have her. Semira whispered to Carmine what was going on. He nodded and smiled nervously. His eyes danced around in confusion, but if Semira said it was time to go, then he was ready to go as well.

"So Semira, who is this handsome man sitting beside you?" Sophina queried as she took a bite of dressing.

Semira was momentarily taken aback because their Momma was taking a plate to Dante. That really grossed Semira out. Hearing her sister's voice, she turned her attention to Sophina and noticed her looking lustfully and longingly at Carmine. Not this time, Semira thought to herself.

She glared at Sophina as to say none of your business, but she knew how her mother was. So she played nice. "This is my boyfriend, Carmine," Semira told her sister.

"Interesting. I can't believe you finally got a man. How did you pull him? Shoot, we thought you would be single forever after Natano. I tell you, Carmine, no man is good enough for her. She's so stuck up sometimes, a real uppity woman. Momma should have named her Saddity," she stated with laughter, recalling how her sister loved to be around the Callaway family.

Sophina thought she was funny, but she was rubbing Semira's last nerve. Semira ignored her. Sophina knew why her sister was single. She knew what she allowed to happen to her and she knew about Natano too. Semira glared at her, and she got the message and turned her attention back to Nalani.

"Nalani, Momma's back. What do you want to do first?" she asked.

Nalani turned her head and burrowed into Semira's chest. She refused to talk to Sophina. Sophina shot Semira the evil eye as if it were her fault. Again, the room grew silent and Nalani buried her head deeper into Semira's chest, her little fingers gripping her sides so tightly Semira had to pull them away. She whispered in her ear to make her feel better.

"Semira, what did you do to my child? Why is she scared of me?" Sophina inquired, her voice loud with irritation. She demanded an explanation.

"Sophina, I don't know what's wrong. It might be the fact that you haven't seen her in years and haven't taken much time with her. Don't you dare accuse me of doing anything. Not this day. You are to blame," Semira snapped with a forced kindness though anger was right beneath. She wrapped her arms around Nalani, who didn't move.

Sophina let out a grunt. "No matter, I'm here now. Nalani, come see Mommy," she coached.

Nalani didn't move. "No. I don't want to see you," she finally replied through tears.

"Sophina, I'm going to take her to rest and when she has had a nap, I'm sure she will talk to you. Just give her some time." Semira picked Nalani up and walked her to the bedroom. She read her a story and let her rest. When she returned, Sophina had sat on the other side of Carmine and was talking to her mother. Semira sat back down and began to nibble and pick at her food. She had lost her appetite that fast. She didn't like Sophina being near Carmine. She knew what had happened with Natano. Sophina ruined anything good for her. It was what she did. Sophina was bitter to the root and miserable, which was why she abhorred seeing another happy.

"Semira, is everything okay with Nalani?" Sophina asked as she was swallowing her turkey.

Semira looked at her, despised by her sight and annoyed with her tone. Sophina's face looked aged, her lips were purple, and her long black hair looked brittle, as if it had not been combed in weeks. Semira couldn't comprehend how she had let a man destroy her beauty. It took a few moments, but she got her thoughts together and replied to her question. "She is resting, and a little upset. You could have called so I could have prepared her for your arrival. I think it would have been better and this situation could have been avoided," Semira explained with a hint of anger. It was hard trying to be sweet and nice when she was upset and irritated with her sister.

"Well, sister, I just wanted to surprise y'all. I didn't know I had to call to see my family," she snidely replied, showing her annoyance with her sister's remark.

Semira was about to reply, but their mother intervened. "Sweetie, we're just happy to have you home," she praised as she clasped her hands, her sable eyes watering. She was just so elated to have Sophina back. It was a prayer she prayed every day and every night.

Semira looked at Carmine. She was ready to go home and take Nalani with her. Sophina only wanted one thing, and that was money. Semira was sure that Dante had put her up to it and she was just simple-minded enough to do whatever he asked. For all she knew, they were casing the place to see what was of value for them to steal.

"Momma, I have to be heading home. I have some work I need to finish. The food was great." Carmine looked at her as if he was surprised by her reaction, but she didn't care. She couldn't sit at that table any longer. One thing that she did not do well was being fake. It wasn't her way.

Ella looked shocked at her daughter's abruptness. She quickly responded, "Honey, don't leave so soon. We still have dessert and we can catch up with your sister."

"Well, Mom, I'm sure I'll have the opportunity to see her. We have to go. Carmine, will you please get Nalani?"

Carmine could tell there were things being said without being said. He could read the body language but now wasn't the time for him to comment. He excused himself and went upstairs.

"Semira," Sophina called, her tone relaxed. "I would like Nalani to stay the night with Momma, so I can be with her."

"Sorry, Sophina, but she has school. I will bring her over here when I get off work," Semira replied coolly. Her sister knew she would never let that happen. Hell would freeze and the devil would have a key before she allowed Sophina to be alone with Nalani. Semira didn't miss the look on her sister's face, but she knew better and so did their mother. They could say whatever they wanted about Semira, but everyone knew when it came to Nalani, her word was final. She was not in the mood for the foolish drama that always followed Sophina. She kissed her dad, brother, Marybeth, and nephew goodbye and walked by Dante like he didn't exist. He irked her in the worst way.

~~~

4. Deonna

Once home, she placed Nalani in bed and she fell fast asleep again. Semira watched her body rest. Her mind wondered why her sister had even come back. *What is she after? It's obvious she is still on drugs and Dante too.* He smelled of alcohol. Semira just had enough. She no longer had the energy to battle Sophina. She would do what was best for Nalani and adopt her. It was the right thing to do. It was the only thing to do. She kissed her once more and said a prayer.

~~~

Carmine came over to take Nalani, Tobias, and Semira out to the Greensboro Children's Museum. Her sister was still in town. Two weeks after her arrival, she lost interest again in seeing Nalani; instead, she was scamming ways to get money. Semira had seen her on the other side of town, possibly pimping out her body to get a quick hit. She was continuing to go down the wrong path. It was heartbreaking to see her older sister fall so far and be so unwilling to accept help.

Semira must have been lost in her thoughts because when she came to, Carmine was staring at her and Nalani was tugging at her shirt. "Sorry. I was in another world. What do you want, Nalani?" she asked sweetly, cupping her face tenderly.

"I wanted to go over there and play," she exclaimed with a smile, her dimples cascading across her face. She looked so much like Natano. Semira smiled back at her and watched her and Tobias run off. Unexpectedly, Carmine grabbed her face, momentarily stunning her, and then he kissed her forehead.

"Babe, just let go and enjoy the day. You and I both know you can't control what your sister does, but you can control your reaction. So stop letting your thoughts drift back to Sophina, and enjoy us."

Semira hated how he knew what was bothering her, but then again, she was not really hiding it. He was right. She was letting things get on her nerves that she didn't have the power to control. "All right, Carmine. You're correct in your mental assessment of me. I'm enjoying the three of you." She needed to talk to him and let him know why she felt like she did, but that would have to wait. The kids deserved to enjoy their day. She had been distant since her sister's return. Seeing her brought back memories, but she shook the thought and enjoyed the day.

~~~

Monday arrived and Mariah, Carmine, Seth, Marybeth, Tobias, Nalani and Semira were inside of the courtroom. It looked like Blaine was not going to make it. Finally, she was going to make their family official. Now, she was adopting her niece to become her mother. She didn't share this with her mother because she would just try to talk Semira out of it. As long as she had Seth's approval, she knew she was doing the right thing. Today was a great day, the best one as Judge Hartfield made it official. They all took pictures together and left the courthouse to go out to a restaurant and let the kids play. "Aunt Se Se, I can call you Momma now," Nalani exclaimed, jumping into her lap and kissing her.

"Yes, if you'd like or you can call me Auntie still. It is whatever makes you feel comfortable," Semira replied, hugging her.

"Okay, I love you!" she gushed.

"I love you too," she intoned and watched her follow Tobias.

"I'm proud of you, sis. You have been taking care of her for a long time. I'm glad you adopted her. I will talk to Mom and Pop about it."

"Forgive me, but is pop your stepdad or biological father?" Carmine asked, again confused.

"Oh, sorry, Carmine. I forgot. We call our biological father by his name, Samson, and we call our stepdad, Pop or Dad. Tobias and Nalani know nothing about Samson. To us, he actually doesn't exist. He was a hard man," she confessed.

Seth shook his head, recalling all the cruel things his father did and how their father had manhandled his sisters. It was the reason Sophina had lost herself so young to men. She wanted approval. She wanted to be loved.

Semira felt Seth's sadness. They'd had a hard life before their momma got remarried, but she finally had a good man who loved all of them.

"Seth, I'm going to take the kids with me tonight. You and Marybeth can have a date night." Semira smiled, winking at Marybeth who was smiling now too.

"I like that. Seth, we need a date night," Marybeth agreed, smiling.

Seth smiled, knowing his sister was trying to change the subject. "We do. Thanks, Semira, for offering to take Tobias."

"There you guys go. I must have gotten the times mixed up. I was at the courthouse looking for you all." Blaine pouted walking toward the dining table.

Semira smiled when she saw him and gave him a hug. "Is your dad here too?" she asked.

"No, he had to go out of town. He is talking to a perspective player. Someone you know well." He grinned.

Semira looked at him curiously as did the rest. She almost forgot her manners. "Blaine, this is Carmine. He's my new beau," she introduced the two. She kind of liked saying that he was hers. It was nice to have a significant other.

"It's nice to meet you. Good job last week. You're a great player," Blaine complimented. Someone had finally gotten Semira's heart.

4. Deonna

"Thank you. So how do you know Se Se?" Carmine asked. He had to know if this guy was checking for his lady. He wasn't an insecure dude, but he knew the woman he had was rare and he wasn't taking any chances.

"She's my best friend. We attended high school and college together. She is exceptionally brilliant. Now, she is running everybody's finances and is a great financial manager, planner, and accountant. If it has to do with numbers and dollars, then you want her on the team. That woman can do great things with money. She ought to be on Wall Street. My dad loves her, we all do," he boasted and winked at Semira.

Semira grew red with embarrassment and she watched her brother nod his head in agreement.

"Carmine, she is good with finances. It was her who kept my momma from economic disaster. She started working at sixteen in the bank and now she is the head of all of it," Seth added.

"She sure is. Oh, and congratulations on adopting Nalani. Where is my little princess? I have some gifts for her in the car," Blaine told them, looking for her.

"She and Tobias are playing games in the game room. You should tell her hello. She'd love to see you," Semira assured him.

"Okay, I will, but first, I have to tell you who Dad is trying to get to play here."

"Who," she asked? She knew it had to be a big name if Mr. Calloway had gone out personally to recruit him.

"Natano Kaholwai, you remember him? He's a great running back and Dad wants him. I told him he should have taken you too, so you can work your magic," he intoned, and with that, he disappeared to find the kids.

Semira dropped her head. *Natano.* She thought she would never see him again. Natano Kaholwai was Nalani's biological father. If he saw her, he would put two and two together. She could not believe that Blaine or Mariah hadn't connected the dots yet. This would not be good, not at all. He needed to stay in Denver where he was playing, and not come to North Carolina. She let out a sigh. This was her worst fear.

"Are you all right?" Carmine asked her, wondering who Natano was. This was the second time his name had come up, and each time she'd had a reaction to it. He wondered had Natano been an ex or something more. She had a serious reaction to his name.

"Yes, I'm fine," she lied.

Darkness fell upon her heart as she thought of all that could occur with the arrival of Natano. She secretly still had feelings for him. Sometimes, she loved him, and other times she

4. Deonna

despised him because he'd offered her a new beginning but quickly shattered her heart when he chose her sister. Sophina was more beautiful than her, more advanced than her, and he found her interesting, but Sophina broke him as he had Semira. He transferred to a school out in California and she hoped that was where he would stay. He got drafted into the NFL and played well, and now Thomas Sr. and Jr. would bring him back here. She just wanted to forget. The rest of the evening seemed to fly by without her participation. Her mind was confused and afraid. The arrival of Natano meant change. She wasn't sure if she was ready for it.

~~~

"Tobias and Nalani, come on so I can tuck you in," Semira yelled downstairs. She could hear them playing with Carmine.

"Can we stay up longer?" they asked.

"No, you have to sleep now. Next week you can stay up late, but not tonight. I'll let you have pizza for breakfast," he compromised. She heard them run upstairs.

"Auntie Se Se," Tobias yelled out of breath. "If you add ice cream, then we have a deal."

"Okay. You each get one scoop but you can't tell your daddy or mommy," she warned.

They shook on it and she tucked them into bed. Carmine read them a story and then they walked downstairs to have adult time.

"Semira, are you okay? All day, you have been distant. I know something is going on in that head of yours." He knew something was up because her eyes looked tired and she had that little worried wrinkle.

She hoped she would never let the words escape her lips. She just wanted to forget it, but it refused to be forgotten. "Carmine, I thought I could date you without my past coming into play, but with my sister back in town and possibly Natano, I have to tell you some things. I have to tell my brother and Mariah too. This is so hard for me. I prayed I never would speak these things," she confessed, not believing she was doing this. She was tired of being trapped by her past. It refused her a future. She wanted there to be no secrets between her and Carmine or anyone for that matter. Secrets were Satan's seeds; they just grew into more sins, more lies, more pains, and more problems. Seven years was too long to keep quiet and it was time to tell the truth.

There was concern in his eyes, almost fear, as he examined Semira, trying to unlock the mystery that had held her captive for far too long. He reached out to her, gently pulled her

4. Deonna

near him, and sat down on the couch. "Semira, tell me what's going on. You're making me nervous."

Her body began to shake uncontrollably. Her mouth opened, but the words would not exit her mouth. They too were afraid. She knew when he found out the truth, this fairytale she was living in would come crashing down. He would view her differently, possibly even judge her. If her drug addicted sister didn't run him off, what she'd allowed to happen to Semira would. "I don't know how to tell you, um, you know I told you I had an issue with men because of my sister and how abusive my father was, but there's more," she confessed uneasily. She wasn't one to give into tears easily, but they were fighting to arrive and she didn't want them to. She needed to be strong as she shared this shame.

"What?" he implored as he tried to calm her. He had never seen someone react the way she was now. What horror was she keeping? It had to be bad as he noted the sheen of sweat on her forehead, the way her eyes watered, and her hands kept moving all over the place. She couldn't be still. She was fidgeting and stuttering out her words.

"What I'm going to tell you, only two people know. Well, my sister knows, but the other person knows only half the story. So you can't tell anyone." She was trying to calm herself. He nodded in agreement. "After my sister gave birth to Nalani, you know I told you she stayed around for a year. She was still using, and one night she brought home her drug dealer, Colt Lampkin. She offered me to him." She noticed the confusion on his face, but she kept on.

"What I mean is, she sold me for crack. I was in my room. I had just put Nalani down. I was getting my nightclothes together and finishing up my homework. He entered my bedroom and he took advantage of me." She suspired to gather her strength. "That night, I lost my virginity to a drug dealer. My own flesh and blood gave me to a man for crack. Everyone thinks I'm so mean and bitter. I guess to some extent I am," she confessed before continuing. "My mom thinks I hate my sister, but I love her so much that I didn't tell. I didn't tell a soul. I never said a thing about it and she never apologized for it. She watched him rape me and didn't try to help. I have never trusted her since. That's why I can never leave her alone with Nalani and why I adopted her. If you don't want me, I understand. I have prepared myself for a life of solitude anyway. I won't be offended if you leave," she finished, looking down at her hands, partially relieved that she had told someone and partially afraid that he would be disgusted with the truth. This was big. It was a huge thing to share. Even Mariah didn't know. It was the first time she allowed herself to be vulnerable and depending on how he reacted, it might be the last.

4. Deonna

He was shocked. Words momentarily left him. It all made sense now. No wonder she didn't want him to be close. There was always hesitation and now he knew why. She had been violated in the worst way that a woman could be. This made him understand her so much better. It explained why she kept Nalani near her, and why she was so worried all the time. It was not anger but a combination of fear and hurt. "I'm sorry, beautiful. How could that ever make me not want you? It was not your fault. I wish I could make you see how truly special and beautiful you are. You should tell your family the truth. You're still hurting. I will do everything in my power to help you and I promise I will never let anyone hurt you or Nalani like that. Never." He could not say more. His words sounded powerless. He wrapped his arms around her and just embraced her. He hated that he had several away games coming. He didn't want to leave her, not now. She was too vulnerable and weak. What she shared with him was raw and gritty. What she needed was his support and comfort and he couldn't provide that and be on the road too.

With tears still in her eyes, she told him there was more. "You remember meeting Blaine and him saying that his father was talking to Natano? Well, Natano is Nalani's birth father, and only Sophina and I know. Natano doesn't know. Sophina was using him and got pregnant. Nalani looks so much like him now. She has his dimples and smile. I worry he will see her and figure it out." She wailed, but she didn't tell him about her history with Natano.

That stunned Carmine. It was almost too much to take in at once, but he cared about both of them. It made sense why she was so stiff when his name was mentioned. She was keeping all kinds of secrets. "He can't do anything because you have adopted her. Do I need to talk to Seth? I mean, is Natano violent? Will he try to hurt you?" he asked, perplexed by the constant flow of information she was giving him. He didn't know how to process it all. It was overwhelming, but he didn't want her to know that. She had enough men in her life betray her and not listen to her. He could not add to that.

"No. He isn't that kind of guy. He's really nice. My sister was the one who wronged him, I guess," she said, recalling how she had fallen for him. "I'm sorry, Carmine. I didn't mean to just tell you all these things. They have been simmering and I just couldn't hide the truth anymore. Again, if this changes anything, I fully understand. I will not be offended at all. I promise."

He looked softly into her eyes. Why was she so sure he would disappear? What was it he was missing? "I'll take care of you. I have to go on the road, but I'll call you every day," he promised as he deepened his embrace, hoping to heal the unsaid sadness that had been eating her for so long.

"Thank you," she whispered. She could not believe how weak she was, how she just told him so much, probably too soon. It was unfair of her to burden him. It felt good not having so many secrets. Now, she had to tell Mariah and Seth too. They knew something was bothering her and she didn't want to lie anymore. She was not sure if she could tell her momma and her dad. She just didn't want to hurt her parents anymore, especially when her mother had such high hopes for Sophina. Semira pondered what she was going to say when she found out about the adoption. There would be some harsh words, probably, and they would be angry with her. That was all right, she supposed. She'd lived that kind of life for a long time, so what did more hurtful words and actions do to someone who was used to the worst anyway? Nothing. She had gotten this far and she would continue to succeed and live her life whether her mother and sister approved or not. She had given them enough of her life, and now she was taking it back. She rested her head on Carmine's chest and closed her eyes.

Chapter 9

The weekend brought somber goodbyes. Semira knew that Carmine would have to travel due to his profession— forty-one games at home, and forty-one games on the road, but he was nearing the end and the playoffs were going to start soon. It was something she was having a hard time dealing with. She guessed because of confessing her secrets and dealing with her sister being around constantly, made her miss Carmine more. Dealing with her mother believing in the lies her sister told her, and Natano coming back to town, was becoming difficult. It was getting harder to be strong when she wanted to be weak and pass the burden on. That was unfair and unjust to try and unload it on Carmine. She had God. Only God could heal those wounds that never seemed to heal.

Nalani and Semira kissed Carmine goodbye and watched him leave. It was like a piece of her was leaving too. She had become too attached to him in a short time. Even when she told herself not to, that if she didn't stop, she would end up brokenhearted. That was her problem. She wanted to be loved, but she was also scared to be loved. Nothing was forever, and even the most respectful of men fell prey to sin. He was a basketball star, a very handsome one, and some women knew no boundaries. With everything else going on in her life, all she could think about after her confession was scaring him right into the arms of another woman. Natano did, so why wouldn't Carmine?

"Well, love, what do you want to do?" Semira asked Nalani with a forced smile. She was still reliving the assault, the adoption, and the possibility of Natano returning. It brought back memories that stung her heart. Natano was her first love and first heartbreak. They had unfinished business, and she wanted him to be so many things, but he turned out to be just another jerk in the line of men who'd failed her. She blamed Sophina too. Everything always went back to Sophina. She was sucking all of the good out of Semira's life, completely ruining her life before she even had a chance to live it.

"I want to eat with you and Auntie Riah," Nalani declared.

Semira called Mariah and asked her to join them for lunch. They needed to talk. She wanted to invite Seth too. She needed to tell them the entire truth. It was time. God knows it was. They both agreed to meet her. She knew Nalani would love to see Uncle Seth and Tobias. They adored each other. Semira and Nalani arrived first and waited for ten minutes for the others to arrive. When Nalani saw Seth's truck, she beamed with excitement. The kids ordered their food and settled in as Semira told Mariah and Seth that she needed to tell them some very important things. She thought they knew it was coming because they were concerned about her, but she was unable to tell them the truth. She had become a different person since the arrival of her sister. Things were closing in on her and she wanted to take her heart back. She was tired of living in a silent shame over a situation that was not her fault. She did everything to help her sister and she did everything to hurt her. What Semira didn't know was why. Lord knows, she could not wait for Sunday. She needed to lay her burdens down. She needed to be around as many godly people as she could find. It was time to confess and let go of the stress. Like Josiah always said, she was too blessed to be depressed.

"What is it, Semira? I know something is wrong," Mariah queried, looking concerned. It was like something horrible took control of her bestie and zapped out all of her energy and kindness. The return of Sophina brought out the worse in Semira. Mariah was confused because she thought Semira wanted her sister to come home.

Semira looked behind her to see what the children were doing. They were watching SportsCenter so she knew they would not hear. She cleared her throat and told them. She didn't cry this time. She had cried so much with Carmine that tears would not form. She saw the shock on both her brother and best friend's faces. It was a pain she hoped never to witness. Their eyes said they would have protected her. She wished her sister had. Life would have been so different if she had not been raped that night.

"Sis, I didn't know. I would have protected you. I remember Colt Lumpkin. They locked him up a few years ago. If he was still around, I'd end him myself," Seth said, feeling furious. First, it was their father, and now this, his sweet little sister sold for crack by Sophina. She was still using. "I'm done with Sophina. She can't even talk to my son or my niece. Sis, I'm so sorry. I didn't have a clue. Are you sure about Natano too?"

Mariah sat silent. They were best friends since grade school. She was supposed to know. Now it seemed so obvious why she would not go to parties or refused to date. She was hurt. All this time, she thought it was because her dad had been so strict, but it was because her innocence was stolen. *How dare he? How dare Sophina?* Then Sophina left her alone to raise a child that was conceived by deceit. Semira went above and beyond for her sister. She was raising her sister's child. Now she understood why Natano transferred from the school. He knew the devilment he'd done.

"I'm sure. I was so mad at Soph for taking him. I thought I loved him and then she came in the room with her model body, long hair, and beauty, and he wanted her. It hurt. I thought I would never get over it. Then she found out she was pregnant. I mean, think about it. Look at Nalani. She looks like him. She has his dimples, his smile, and his charm. She swore me to secrecy. He never knew about her. He transferred back to USC in California. Then after that, she sold me. Now she's here and I feel like that girl again, especially when Momma is falling at her feet. It hurts me. I don't know what to do," Semira confessed.

"Se Se, don't worry about it. You are the best thing that ever happened to Nalani. Your mother knows that too. Everything will work out for the best, you'll see. Besides, Natano probably won't even come here," Mariah said, still in disbelief. That had to be the worst thing to raise a child that came from her sister and her first love, to wake up each day loving a child that was the reflection of betrayal. How had she done it and kept it a secret?

"He is. I got a call from Mr. Calloway. He confirmed and wants me to meet with him. Tuesday morning, I have a meeting with Natano and I don't know what to do," she whispered.

"Sis, Mariah is right. God will work this out. I mean, taking Natano out of the equation, are you al lright, you know, about what happened? Marybeth can see you if you need to talk," he offered.

4. Deonna

"I'm good. I was seventeen back then and I have done just fine. I don't need therapy. I just needed to be honest with the people I love and who love me."

"What about Mom and Pop. Are you going to tell them too?" Seth questioned.

"Later. Right now, there is a lot to deal with. Sophina is still around. I saw her working the streets and with Dante pulling her strings, who knows what will happen. I'm more worried about Sunday dinner than anything," Semira confessed.

"No need, I will take care of you, sis. Leave Mom to me about the adoption and Sophina. Pop doesn't want Sophina and Dante there either, so I'll just have Sunday dinner at my house. Sophina won't come there. She knows better," he said, sipping his tea and trying to fight the tears that were trying to release themselves. He could not comprehend his sister selling her baby sister so she could get a hit. She'd do the same thing to Nalani or even Tobias if given the chance. "Sis, if you don't mind, I'd like to take Nalani and Tobias to the movies," he said.

Semira thought that was a kind gesture, especially since the children loved being together and they loved Seth. "I don't mind, but I thought you might want me to take them so you and Marybeth could do something," she said.

"We like spending time with them. We need to get used to two," he gushed.

"Are you guys pregnant again?" Semira asked. Her face lit up as she thought of the prospect of having another niece or nephew. Semira loved children so much.

"Yes," he chortled with equal joy on his face.

"Great, I love babies. I can't wait!" she exclaimed, getting up and hugging him. It made her feel better about everything. A new birth was what the family needed, what they all needed. Sometime in July or August, a new baby would be joining the family. She loved that. She loved that so much.

~~~

Tuesday came too quickly. The week started stressfully and Semira prayed it would not end that way. Unfortunately, the dinner at Seth's house didn't go as planned. Their mother brought Sophina and Dante, against the wishes of everyone. Since she was unaware of the past, she thought she was doing right. Semira was unable to share the news that she'd adopted Nalani. They did celebrate that Marybeth was pregnant again. An argument ensued, which caused Seth to put Dante and Sophina out, and Ella had followed, leaving their father behind. He said that Ella had allowed Dante and Sophina to come in and out of the house. Now he dreaded going home. So he moved in with Semira and Nalani for a while until things settled down a bit. Nalani loved that as did Semira.

4. Deonna

It was time for her to let him know the things that haunted her. They talked. They talked about the adoption, and the unspeakable thing her sister had done to her. She saw the same hurt in him that she had seen in Seth. She hated that look, that feeling. He only wished she'd told him sooner so he could have protected her, as Seth had said. She just wanted to protect Nalani. She wanted to shield her from everything, but it was so hard to do when her sister was the one she was protecting Nalani from. Her mind was deeply embedded in the thoughts of the past few weeks that she almost forgot about having a meeting. She glanced at her watch briefly and a voice caught her attention.

"I'm not late. I still have five minutes," she heard a familiar voice say. Then she smelled him. He smelled so lovely, looked so lovely, and those dimples that had once melted her heart did so again. Why did he have that impact on her? She didn't know. The years had been kind to him. He still took exceptional care of himself. He was groomed to perfection. For a moment, she went back in time, back to when she'd first met him and they connected instantly. He had been the best thing, until Sophina. Why he'd wanted her sister, a dropout with a drug addiction, had been far beyond her. She had her theories.

"Semira, my-oh-my, you are just as lovely as ever. You are more beautiful than I remember. When did you fill out like

162

that?" he complimented, placing out his hand to pull her up and hug her.

She stopped him mid-stride. "Enough, Natano, let's get to business. Mr. Calloway said you were looking to change management. So how can I assist you?" she asked, not allowing her emotions to get her hooked like they had her freshman year of college. When she was green, naïve, innocent, and in love with this man. He may have forgotten, but she hadn't and she was going to deflate his ego.

"Mira, this is me, Natano. You don't have to act all business with me. We're friends," he reminded her, sitting down, smiling at her, and instantly flirting.

She hadn't been called Mira in a long time. Only he'd called her that, but she ignored him. Friends? How dare he call himself a friend? They hadn't spoken since he'd chosen her sister over her. She didn't understand his definition of the word. "I thought this was a meeting. When I have clients, I get to business. However, if this is a social call, I have better things to do with my time. I have important clients and a great deal of work. I did this because Mr. Calloway is a dear friend. What is it you need?" she asked sharply, again not cracking a smile and not being at all sweet. There was no Mariah here, so she didn't have to pretend. She was still hurt by his treatment and his reappearance solved nothing.

4. Deonna

"Okay," he replied. She was no longer bashful and he liked it. She was a take-charge kind of gal. "Wow, you have changed from the sweet little timid freshman. You are truly about the business. Look, I know it has been a long time since we talked, but I feel a little hostility, and I don't want it to be that way."

"I apologize if I came off too frank. I'm, as you say, about my business. So if you would like to deal with us, let me get your signatures. As far as college, that was years ago and deeply in the past where I plan to let it stay," she snapped, pulling out the papers from her Brahmin briefcase.

"Mira, I'll sign anything you ask me to. I trust you. I know you. I know how highly everyone speaks of you. I also know when things didn't work out between us, and how my behavior hurt you. It changed you. If I had been as mature then as I am now, I would have chosen you. I got caught up in the life. Sophina was exciting and fun and I was led by flesh and not by faith. I wish I had been a more mature Christian back then, but I am now. I would like your forgiveness and have the opportunity to be a better friend to you," he earnestly confessed.

Semira was not prepared for this. She hoped he would have forgotten about her, married and moved on. It would have been easier. No. Here he was. He was fine as wine, being humble and apologizing for his actions. Her stupid heart soaked it up like she'd be in a love drought. If there was ever a question about her being over him, she had her answer now. "Okay, you're forgiven and it is forgotten, but I really am short on time," she told him, feeling like a school girl. He embodied her innocence and he reminded her of the happiness she used to have until he and her sister broke her heart. For so long she blamed herself, saw all of her imperfections and flaws, and buried her pain as if her feelings didn't matter. She cared so deeply for family and friends and she felt like she got back less than she gave. She wanted to go back in time and rewrite the history that was now permanently part of her life.

He felt embarrassed by his past actions, but she was everything Mr. Calloway said and so much more. Even in her business attire and professional attitude, she was still sweet and caring. Always wanting to please and smooth things over. After he'd transferred and went back home to California, he'd thought of her always. Seeing her now made him want her all over again. He wished he could rewrite history. "I understand. Maybe I can visit you later this week. Me, you, Blaine, and whomever he is dating this week and Mariah. Is she married yet?"

"No, she is still playing the field and breaking hearts," Semira confessed in a less sharp tone.

4. Deonna

He smiled at that. "She's pretty. She can flip a man around, break his heart, mend it and break it again. She was a lot of fun," he teased, recalling the good days.

"She still is a lot of fun and a dear friend to me," she warned in a tone that said don't go too far. He was not back in her good graces.

"I heard you changed, and that you have broken some hearts yourself. Though I can't see you breaking anyone's heart. He said that these athletes love you and you shut them down. I thought, not sweet Mira. She goes to class, to the library to study and to church. You have transformed, no longer hiding behind glasses, hats, and big clothes. Please forgive my bluntness, but you are breathtaking. I hear you are doing big things, got a nice house, two very expensive cars, debt free, and a daughter."

She was taken aback by his knowledge of her life, as well as his blunt flirting with her. "Who has been feeding you all this information?" she demanded as a frown etched her face. She bet it was Blaine.

"Well, when Thomas Calloway found out that I knew you, he told me and his son, Thomas Jr. how much they love you. Mr. Calloway said he bought you a Mercedes-Benz for helping him with his finances. Then he said that you adopted a

166

daughter. I remember you saying you wanted to do that. Saint Semira, saving the world one child at a time."

She seldom drove that expensive car. Mr. Calloway insisted she take it. She bought a nice house in a nice community because Nalani deserved that. She wanted her to have a different life than her own upbringing. They had good neighbors who cared about one another. There were no drug dealers there, and the police came faster there than in her old neighborhood. "It's just stuff and doesn't mean that much to me." She was not a materialistic person. Things had no value to her, but honor, integrity, respect, now that counted to Semira.

"I know it doesn't. You are a woman of humility. Do you have any pictures of this little darling?" he asked, admiring how lovely Semira was. She looked so sophisticated and professional now, so in contrast of what he remembered. She was still cautious and still sweet but different. She had always been a classy woman. There was no one like her, and he missed her dearly.

She did, but she didn't want him to see, not until he knew the truth. "Listen, we can talk about that later, but I have to get back to work," she reminded.

"I understand, but can I call you? I really want to see you and get the gang together."

4. Deonna

"Yeah, I guess. My number is the same as it was back in college," she said. He smiled. She left the idea of explaining that her adopted child was his daughter to herself. She was not ready to tell Nalani that Natano was her father. That was going to take some time. She returned back to work and pretended nothing was wrong. She sent Mariah and Seth an email. She needed some advice and she needed to pray. She needed God to show her what to do. She hadn't been prepared for this to happen. They both deserved to know the truth. There was never a good reason to keep a secret or tell a lie. Now the past was coming up so quickly it had to come out. There was never a good time to reveal these truths but she was going to do it. She was just going to have to do it and deal with the consequences.

~~~

Blaine drove Natano around the area to reacquaint him. It had been awhile since Natano had been in North Carolina. They talked about the old days and how much fun college had been. Natano wanted to steer the conversation to Semira and find out what had been going on since he left so many years ago.

"Dude, look, there goes Sophina. At least, she looks a little better than when she first arrived," Blaine commented, shaking his head. She had gone from prom queen to hot mess. It was sad to see someone so lovely and talented throw her life away for drugs and bad boys. He was a firm believer that God could turn a mess into a masterpiece.

"Are you sure? That can't be Sophina. She looks so bad," Natano replied in shock.

"I know. Doing drugs and drinking will do that to you. Semira doesn't like to talk about it much. I can see why. Not only is she physically different, but her spirit is sick," Blaine confessed.

"Tell me because I have no idea. After the meeting I had with Semira, I have more questions than answers," he told him, recalling it all in his head.

"She's been through a lot. After you left, her sister gave birth to a baby, Nalani. She's a doll. I spoil her rotten every chance I get. She calls me Uncle Blaine because I'm her godfather and Mariah is her godmother. Anyway, she was born prematurely because Sophina was on and off drugs while she was pregnant. Sophina just abandoned the baby and left Semira to take care of her. She did, and she did it well. She stayed on the dean's list even though she was working and taking care of the baby, and got a competitive internship. Sophina put her through it. From bringing drug dealers and her drug buddies to just stealing from her sister. Semira made it and finished undergraduate and graduate school in five years. She has been moving up ever since. I look at Semira and I'm in awe at how

4. Deonna

she rose above her situation," he said, turning to the left and heading toward Semira's house. "I'm going to show you where she lives," he said. He was proud of her and what she accomplished. She didn't complain, she just worked super hard. That had come from her paternal side indeed.

Natano listened intensely. The name Nalani was the name he wanted to name his first daughter, after his grandmother who passed away his senior year of high school. He remembered sharing that with Semira. "So is Nalani the child that Semira adopted?" he asked for clarification.

"Yes, her sister's child," Blaine confirmed, slowing down as they reached her subdivision. "This is her house. She has really done well for herself."

"Yes, it looks like it. Is she at home?" Natano asked. He wanted to know more about Nalani.

"Nah, she is probably somewhere with Nalani. She's the best mother. If I ever get married, I want my wife to be a mother like Semira. She's great. She's a natural. You would never know that Semira didn't birth Nalani. I just hope Carmine will be a good father figure."

"Who is Carmine?"

"He's the guy Semira is dating," Blaine replied.

Dating? Not that he expected her to be single, but this was a surprise to him. Semira didn't reveal that information, nor had she told him about Nalani. *What happened to Sophina?* There were a million things swarming in his head. *What had he walked into? What secret or secrets was she keeping from him?* "Blaine, do you have her contact number?" he asked.

"I do. When I drop you off, I will give it to you. She still has the same number from college."

He nodded. She did tell him that. "What else is she doing?" he asked.

"Everything. She is all over. People know her all across North Carolina because she helps so many needy families, and is so active with the church. It's like she never stops. I think sometimes she works so hard because of what she has been through. Mariah can tell you better. Those two are joined at the hip. I've been thinking about asking Mariah out, but I'm not sure if I'm her type," he confessed.

Natano was too distracted to respond. His mind was too busy trying to make connections. "B, how old is Nalani?"

"I think she's seven. Dude, did you not hear me about Mariah?"

"Sorry, yeah you should ask her out. I was thinking we could all get together. We can have a little cookout and invite them," he said, adding on his fingers. He did have relations with Sophina and it could be that Nalani was his, but Semira would have told him if that were so. Or would she? He did break her

4. Deonna

heart and just walked out like their friendship and relationship meant nothing, but it had. They were basically an item until he saw Sophina. It was the only thing he ever regretted doing, leaving her without an explanation or expressing his feelings.

"Natano, I like that idea. I'll call and do that. We can invite some of the football players too."

"Right," he agreed, thinking how he was going to talk to Semira about the news. Maybe he should just show up at her house and ask, but that might be too forward. He had to know, and he could not rest until the questions in his head were answered.

"Natano, are you all right? I have been talking to you and it's like you have not heard anything that I said."

"Sorry. I was in another place."

~~~

Finally, Semira was finished at work and headed to Seth's house to pick up Nalani. Since her sister was in town, she was uncomfortable leaving her at church. She was afraid their momma might pick her up and let her spend time with Sophina. Semira could not allow that. She pulled into the driveway and saw Nalani and Tobias outside playing. She recalled when she was that young. When she was seven, her sister ten, and their brother thirteen, and how miserable life was. Samson was always mad about something or telling them what they could not do, and Momma was trying to please him, but she never could. She had a thing for a lost cause. She was the same way with Sophina, knowing how Daddy didn't like having her there. God had given her mother a better husband and she was allowing her drug addicted daughter to ruin it. Semira didn't understand the women in her family, why they felt it necessary to push good men away and hold on to the bad ones. Not her. She made a promise to herself not to be who they were. She would not teach Nalani those skills either. She was so glad that Nalani never knew Samson, because he was a horrible man with a short temper. The abuse they all had to suffer and see, she would give her life to make sure nothing like that ever touched Nalani or Tobias.

She parked the car, got out, and began to play with Tobias and Nalani. They made life bearable. The sweet innocence of youth, innocence she'd lost long ago if she ever had it. In them, she saw life again. She smiled and laughed and saw as they saw. That was what Samson stole from her and her siblings. All that she achieved didn't fill or heal the hurt, didn't stop the longing and didn't stop the nightmares. *Why did she not see how troubled her sister was? Why did she allow herself to be hurt by her continuously? Why did she have to be the bad one, addicted to all the sins they learned not to do in Sunday school?* It made no sense to Semira. Sophina was always

4. Deonna

creating messes and Semira was always trying to clean them up. Now with the return of Natano, she was going to have to tell him, but how? It was a conversation she didn't want to have. It was an issue that she should not have to even deal with. Still, seven years later, Sophina was interrupting her life. She was growing tired of it. It was time to let her and Momma know she'd adopted Nalani. She was not going to keep any more secrets. She was going to talk with Natano too. It was going to be difficult, but he deserved to know as well.

"All right you two, come on inside so I get Nalani's things and talk to your momma," Semira said to them. They followed her as she opened the door.

Semira found Marybeth in the kitchen and gave her a hug. "Thank you for keeping Nalani for me," she said.

"No problem, I was glad for the company. Seth told me that under no circumstances was I to take either of them to your mother's while your sister is in town," she said.

"Yeah, I agree. It just isn't safe, especially with Dante around. I wish momma would make them leave. It isn't safe for her either. When Sophina is using she can't think clearly. She'll do anything, just unspeakable horrible things."

Marybeth noticed this and placed her hand on top of hers. "I'm here if you need to talk," she offered.

Semira wondered if her brother told her after she asked him not too. She appreciated her sentiment, but she took care of herself. "Thanks, but I'm good. Nalani and I need to be getting home. I have to start dinner," Semira told her, turning around and meeting Nalani at the end of the stairs. She hugged Tobias and kissed his cheek. She said goodbye and she and Nalani were off. Nalani talked a mile a minute about her day and how much fun she had with Tobias, and then she asked about Carmine. He and Semira were having a hard time catching one another, but they emailed and texted each other daily. Semira would make sure Nalani got to talk to him before bed tonight. She really liked Carmine, and it made Semira feel guilty. Nalani needed a father, and for seven years due to her own selfishness, Nalani was denied the chance to know her biological father.

"Come on, sweet pea," she coaxed, opening the door for her. When she returned home, she noticed her dad's car was not at home, so she figured he had gone to see Momma.

"Where is Papaw?" Nalani asked.

"He is probably at home with G-Momma. Would you like to call him?" Semira questioned, placing her briefcase down.

"No, that's okay. I have some homework to do."

Semira opened Nalani's bookbag, read her assignment, and got her set up to start work. She then began to cook and

175

prepare for the rest of the week. She heard the doorbell ring and ran to the door. She knew it was Mariah because she liked to play a tune with the doorbell. Semira opened the door and Mariah walked inside and gave her a hug.

"Where is the cutest kid in America?"

"She is doing her homework, and I'm cooking. Come on and make yourself at home," Semira replied.

"Listen, you will not believe who phoned me today," she told her.

Semira couldn't. She could not remember all of her men. "Who, because after you tell me I have to tell you about Natano,"

"Blaine called me. He said he was having a cookout for Natano and wanted me and you to come. The weird thing is, and I know this will sound crazy, but I felt like he was coming on to me," she confessed, taking off her shoes.

"Really? Well, you are attractive, smart, and on your grind all the time, so I don't think that is crazy," Semira replied. She would never have thought about the two of them since Mariah liked dark men and not white ones, but Blaine had swagger and he was fine.

"You think that he is into me? If it were you, I'd believe it. He loves you and always has, but me? I don't know."

Semira laughed. Mariah never reacted this way about a guy. Semira and Blaine were not meant to be. They were great friends, like sister and brother. She was not into Blaine in that way. "I don't think so," she replied, walking back into the kitchen and looking to see if Nalani needed help, but she was doing well without her assistance.

"Well tell me about the blast from our past," she asked in code.

"He basically apologized about the past. He starts flirting with me. Mr. Calloway and TJ told him my entire life story including my adopting Lani."

"Oh," she intoned looking sadly, before continuing. "What are you going to do?" she asked, pouring herself some tea and sitting down beside Nalani, who was now looking at them.

"I'm going to tell the truth."

Mariah looked shocked but didn't say anything. Semira could tell Nalani was trying to understand what was going on. Semira was relieved when the phone rang. She picked up the phone that was in the kitchen. The voice made her smile. Carmine had the most pleasant voice. She told him that Nalani wanted to talk to him. Nalani leapt off the chair and charged toward the phone. She told Carmine all the things he missed since he had been on the road. Semira went back to making

4. Deonna

turkey spaghetti, garlic bread, and salad. While Carmine was on the road, Semira was learning how to make homemade pasta. She hoped by the time he came back home that she would have mastered it. Italian foods and southern foods were different, but they both made you feel the same. There was love and an art to making good food. "Momma, Carmine wants to talk to you," Nalani called out.

Hearing her call her momma never got old. It was the best name to be called, and Semira loved hearing her say it. It warmed her heart. She picked up the phone and just listened to his voice. She wanted to tell him about Natano, but he was so excited about how well they were doing on the road, and talking to Nalani, that she didn't have the heart to bring up that kind of news. She listened intently as he spoke. She told him she would call him before she went to bed. She wanted to finish cooking dinner to feed Mariah and Nalani; both of them looked like they were ready to eat.

"It is time to eat," she yelled, sitting their plates before them. Nalani said grace, and Semira liked to hear her say it. They learned that at church. They ate, and she listened to Mariah talk about her day, as well as Nalani.

"Semira, thanks again for feeding me. That was good. I mean, really good. I'll see you two at church tomorrow, God willing." she said, but before she left she gave Nalani a big hug and kiss.

"Bye, Auntie Riah," Nalani said singsong and waving.

"Come on, sweet pea, you need to take a bath and get your pajamas on. Then we can watch a movie," Semira said and they walked upstairs together.

4. Deonna

Chapter 10

Semira let out an exhaustive sigh as she sat down at her home office and opened the internet browser. She had a million things to deal with and she just wanted to read random blogs and laugh at other peoples' problems. Mariah had told her about a site that talked about basketball players and she wanted to see if Carmine was on there. She didn't see anything, just some old stuff about him being traded. So she Googled his name, something she should have done the very first time she met him, but she didn't. It was shocking what she discovered. He seemed to be having a really good time on the road. Semira knew that he told her he was a Christian man and over his wild days, but this photo indicated differently. He was coming out of a strip club with two women hanging on his arms. He was called, *Pontiero the Playboy*. That was a shock to her. She felt those old feelings returning when Natano had chosen Sophina and left her. Was Carmine going to do the same thing too? It didn't matter. She was stupid. She should have known better. That was why she could not contact him because he was busy with all his women. She told Mariah this was how it was going to play out.

She collected all the information. When he returned home, they would have a conversation about this, or maybe she would just release him. She would not allow his immature behavior to negatively impact Nalani. Since he had been on the road, she had done just fine without him. Even better than fine, she was doing superbly. He'd fooled her for sure. Pretending to be concerned when the entire time he had been partying, he acted like playing ball occupied his every moment. But from the photos, it looked like other things were occupying his time. They were not married and he was free to do as he pleased. So was she.

~~~

She looked at her calendar and could not wait. One more week and Carmine would be home because he would have some serious explaining to do. She got into the shower and just let the water cascade down her back. The steam seemed to revitalize her. She had a lot to do, so much to say, and she wondered how to start the conversation with her momma and her sister. Each time she tried to tell her momma, something happened, or she chickened out. She didn't want to deal with the aftermath she knew would occur. Their mother loved Sophina, and it seemed more than she did Semira or Seth. No matter what Sophina did, Momma made an excuse and had an unshakeable faith in her. Semira tried not to let it impact her. She had Nalani, Mariah, Seth, Tobias, Pop and Blaine. They had faith in her and loved her. That should be enough. It would have to be. Her mother had chosen sides and Semira, like always, was left alone. Now, she didn't even have Carmine's support. Why was she so trusting of the wrong people? Why did she always hush that inner voice that warned her? Not again. After this, she would not do that to herself again. It was dangerous. It was time to go back to the single life.

"Momma, are you done yet? I want to go to G-Momma's house," Nalani requested.

Semira smiled at her request. "We will go. Just let me put on some clothes. Have you finished dressing?" she asked through her closed door.

"Yes, ma'am, but you have to do my hair," she said through the door.

"I will. Give me about ten minutes," she responded and began to dress. As soon as she walked out of the bathroom, she heard her cell phone. She knew it wasn't Carmine because that was not his ringtone. She picked up the phone but didn't recognize the number. "Hello?"

"Mira, it's me Natano. I wanted to know if I could see you today," he asked.

"Well, um, well maybe later. I have to take Nalani to my parents' house," she said.

"I remember how to get to her house. I can come over," he suggested, being persistent. He had some questions that he needed the answers to.

She didn't want him to. She had to meet him at the cookout that Blaine was having today that was as much interaction as she wanted. "Can't we just talk when I come over to Blaine's?" she asked.

"Well, we can go together. I want to know about Nalani," he said.

She wondered what he knew. That was the name he'd wanted to name his daughter, and when she was born, Semira had to name her that. She never thought it would come back to haunt her. She figured she was going to kill two birds with one stone. "You can come, I guess," she said, stammering over the words.

"Thank you."

"You might as well just come to my house. Do you know where I live?"

"I do. I'm coming now."

She hung up the phone and looked at her Bible. "Dear God, please give me courage and strength," she requested.

"Mommy, my hair," Nalani whined, standing at her door holding her brush.

Semira fixed it for her. Her hair was long and raven just like Sophina's, and she had curly locks like Natano's. Semira wondered how she should tell Nalani about Natano—maybe he would not care. Maybe he would be like Sophina and just not be affected. She would know soon enough.

"Nalani, a friend of mine is coming over. You have not met him before, but be nice to him for me?" she asked, kissing her forehead.

She nodded in agreement, and Semira went upstairs to finish getting ready. As she was fixing her hair, she sent a text to Mariah and her brother hoping they would give her some encouragement. The truth was always better no matter what. She could not teach Sunday school and live a lie. Just as she put on her shoes, the doorbell rang. She ran down the stairs with Nalani behind her.

"Is he your friend, mommy?" Nalani asked her.

"Yes, this is Natano. He's a professional football player," Semira explained to her.

"Cool! It's nice to meet you Natano. My mommy has the coolest friends," she bragged, her missing teeth now growing back. He looked at her and smiled, and then looked at Semira.

"She is beautiful and very sweet," he commented, looking at her curly hair and dimples. She favored him so much.

"Come inside," Semira offered. As he walked in, she saw Mariah pulling up and was thankful. She could keep Nalani occupied while she had the talk with Natano. Boy, was she feeling jittery and nervous. It wasn't like she had done anything wrong, but still. It was beating on her brain about what she was going to have to tell him. She tried not to look at him, but that was near impossible.

"Mommy, look, Auntie Riah is coming. Oh boy, we have a lot of company today. Can I go to her?" she asked.

"You sure can. Then you can show her the new American doll you got. Mariah loves dolls as much as you do," Semira said as she watched her run out to greet Mariah. Semira gave Mariah a wave and she nodded. She and Mariah had that thing that twins have. They communicated without words just knew one another that way.

"Is she mine?" he inquired. "I'm sorry. I played this over and over in my head and I didn't mean to sound so brash."

His words penetrated her ears. It surprised her. She was not aware he was going to be so straight forward. She looked into his eyes and spoke. "It's okay. She is your biological child. You can see that yourself. She has your hair, dimples, and smile," Semira confessed, walking him inside.

"I didn't know," he confessed. All this time he had a daughter and he never knew. She looked like his twin. She was beautiful and perfect. The person he hurt most in this world was raising his child.

4. Deonna

"I didn't either until my sister had her and told me. I named her Nalani and that was it. You were in California and never contacted me. My sister left, so I just raised her as my own. I just recently adopted her. I wasn't trying to hide it from you. I didn't think you'd care. You didn't care about me."

"Look, don't think that I want anything from you. I have been taking care of us financially since she has been in this world," she intoned, recalling how he'd treated her previously. She could take him dismissing her, but not hurting Nalani. Not as long as there was breath in her body would she allow anyone to harm her daughter. That included him. God knows he hurt her deeply.

The honesty hurt. He could see her relive the pain as she spoke. She was a better person than he had ever imagined. "I was not the most mature person back then. I would have been for her and you. Your sister—" he tried to say.

She stopped him. "I don't want to hear it. It doesn't matter. It's in the past, buried, done and gone. So just come on and let's go. I have to take Nalani to see my momma and daddy. Today is the day secrets will be revealed. I have to tell my momma I adopted Nalani because she doesn't know," she explained, getting ready to walk to the door.

"Wait, please just wait. I made a mistake that night, and when I saw the look of hurt in your eyes, I felt horrible. I ran away because I couldn't face you," he replied honestly, reaching out to her. It was obvious to him that she was still hurting. He wanted to make it right. No matter how long it took, he was going to make it right and earn Semira's trust and love.

The touch of his hand on her exposed skin sent unknown feelings throughout her body. Feelings she had never felt, even when Carmine touched her. It was the touch from him that she had longed for. Natano still could make her weak; however, she could not allow herself to slip, not now. She had been so strong for so long. If she allowed herself to fall under his spell again, he would only break her heart. She was done with heartbreak. "Okay, so we were all young and we all make mistakes. It's done," she stated, trying not to showcase any feelings or reveal how wounded she was. She had been strong too long to fall apart now. He would not have the satisfaction of knowing how deeply she loved him and then longed for him when he left. It was a deep-seated agony that made her bitter about relationships.

Her words said so much more. He'd wronged her. It tore him apart inside knowing the pain he caused. "I hurt you, and I never wanted to do that. Now knowing for the past seven years you have been raising my child because of my carelessness, well it just shows how good you are and how I'm not. I want to be there for her and you," he told her, placing his hands softly

4. Deonna

on her arms in an attempt to pull her into his chest to embrace her.

She shook her head and stretched her arms out to separate them. "I can't do this right now. Don't come in here all charming. You laid with my sister in my apartment. I cared about you. I supported you, and you made your choice. I accept the apology and I forgive you, but I can't forget it. I thought I could, but I can't. It's over and there is no reason to relive it. I'm going to my parents. I'll see you at Blaine's house," she quipped, walking to the door and rushing by him. She didn't want his hug. She didn't want to care anymore. She just didn't want to care.

"Can I come too?" he asked. He was not going to miss any opportunity to be with the one he still loved and his daughter.

Semira didn't want him to, but she said he could. They all got into her Mercedes-Benz. She only drove it to Calloway functions since Mr. Calloway had bought it for her. It made him feel good when he saw her driving it around. Natano sat in the front and Mariah sat in the back with Nalani. Semira hoped Seth was coming too. She had a feeling she would need him. They pulled up to her mother's house. She saw Sophina in the backyard. She figured Dante was lurking somewhere. Sophina didn't recognize Semira's car but when she got out, her face brightened a little. Semira got Nalani out and held her tightly in her arms. She was glad that she and Mariah were working out because a few months ago, she'd be too heavy for Semira to carry, but not now. It was not a stress at all. When Nalani saw Sophina, she held Semira even tighter. Semira understood how she felt. Just a few minutes later, Seth pulled up as well. Momma came to the door hearing all the car doors shut and she stood on the porch smiling. Nalani and Tobias raced one another to get to her.

"My grandbabies. Y'all come on and let me spoil you both. All my children are here too. I'm so happy. I missed y'all. Hey, Mariah, I have not seen you in a while. Come and give me a hug too," she requested. "Now who is this handsome young man?" she asked, looking at Natano.

He smiled and offered her his hand. "I'm Natano. I'm an old friend of Semira and Mariah," he introduced with a sweet smile. It was the first time he had ever met their mother, and she was just as beautiful and as lovely as her daughters.

"Okay, nice to meet you," came her quick reply as she eyed him long and hard. Something 'bout that boy looked familiar. Nalani and he kinda favored. He was a handsome young man. She never recalled Semira ever speaking of him. Lately, her daughter was bringing some good-looking young men around, she hoped Semira was going to get married soon and give her more grandbabies.

"Momma, I need to talk to you," Semira spoke in an even tone as she saw Sophina come around to the front the house.

Sophina stopped in her tracks when she saw Natano, and in an instant, everything flooded her brain: their relationship, her sister seeing them, and the daughter she bore because of that sin. She felt a shame she had never felt before. She had taken her sister's boyfriend on purpose and now she was reliving that moment. "Nat, what are you doing here?" she asked, wondering if he knew about Nalani.

He turned and looked at her. She had changed and aged. "I'm accompanying your sister. We have a cookout to get to after this so I'm just tagging along. How are you?" he asked, walking toward her and holding out his hand to shake hers. She didn't look the same as she had years ago. Her beauty seemed to have faded.

She avoided his hand and instantly felt ashamed at how she looked. "I'm good," she replied flatly.

"Well, Sophina, baby what's the matter? You act like you have seen a ghost. Are you all right?" Ella asked, noticing the awkwardness between Sophina and Natano.

"Yeah, Momma I'm fine." she assured, giving Semira an evil stare.

"Well y'all come inside the house," she said opening the door for everyone to enter.

Seth held Semira's hand. He knew she needed support, and his being there gave her strength that she needed. Once inside, Marybeth got the kids and took them into the kitchen.

"Semira, what is it you want to tell me? I feel like it is something major the way you looking," she intoned, sitting down.

"Well, you know how I have been talking about adopting Nalani."

"What? You can't do that," Sophina interrupted.

"Sophina, hush and let your sister finish. You can sit down beside me," Ella ordered.

Daddy looked and shook his head. "Ella, you listen to this child and don't interrupt. You don't say anything either Sophina," he said, looking sternly at her.

She rolled her eyes. He was not her father, and he was not going to tell her what to do.

"Well, Momma, I adopted Nalani. It's official and she is legally my child," Semira confessed, feeling another weight being lifted from her. However, the look of shock on both her mother and sister's faces was not a surprise.

4. Deonna

"How dare you, Semira? I trusted you to care of her not to take her from me. She ain't yours. She is mine," she yelled.

Semira saw Mariah leave to see if the children heard, but Marybeth had already taken them outside. "Sophina, she isn't yours. You have never been there for her. You abandoned us. She is mine. I have raised her since she came from your womb and you know that," Semira snapped. "It was me sitting up late when she screamed and cried for hours. It was me taking her to scheduled doctor's appointments and she had many. The first year of her life was hard. I took care of her. I did what you refused to do."

"Semira, you could have talked to me. I told you not to do that. I told you to wait and let Sophina work out her problems. How dare you bring this young man here and put out our family business like that? I'm ashamed of your behavior," Ella fussed, shaking her head.

"Now, Ella, you are wrong for that, just wrong. All Semira did was take care of Sophina's responsibilities like always," Josiah heatedly stated.

"Momma, he is family. Ask Sophina who he is," Semira quipped, becoming highly agitated.

She looked stunned. "Semira you promised," she fumed, growing angry with her sister.

"I know, but I never thought he would come back. Momma, he is Nalani's biological father," she confessed.

"What? I thought you said you didn't know," she said, looking at Sophina. He looked like Nalani because he was one-half of her. This was why Sophina and Semira had been at odds. They were fighting over a guy.

"He left, Momma. I just didn't think about it," she defended. "Momma, she stole Nalani from me. You said if I got rid of Dante that I could have her back," she said, looking at Ella.

Semira shook her head. How could she do that, and to her no less? Momma knew Sophina was not ready to raise a child. It was not her place to tell Sophina that. Even now, in the midst of all the dirt her sister had done, the mistakes she was continuously making, and her childish behavior, their mother was still siding with her. The one who never listened, never respected authority and did whatever she wanted when she wanted. They deserved each other, Semira thought angrily to herself.

"Well, I didn't know that your sister was sneaking behind my back. You two should not be fighting over some guy. I don't care how handsome he is. Semira, what were you thinking? I raised you better than that. You are supposed to look after your sister. You have connections. You could have gotten her a job or something useful, not take her child from her. It was wrong and you know it," she fussed, raising her voice.

Seth let out a frustrated sigh. "It was the right thing to do. If you knew what Sophina did to Semira you'd understand," he exploded. He was so tired of the excuses made for Sophina. She was dangerous and didn't deserve to be a mother. It wasn't like she wanted to be anyway.

Ella shook her head. "It doesn't matter. It's wrong and she's wrong," she snapped.

Seth opened his mouth to defend his sister.

"Don't Seth, don't do it. She has a right to her opinion," Semira stated.

"Mrs. Irving, you are wrong. You shouldn't talk to Semira like that," Mariah defended, feeling her anger rise. That was her best friend, her sister girl, and no one was going to talk to her like that. Especially, after all she had suffered in silence; not even her own blood was going to attack her. Mariah was not going to back down.

"You just mind your business," Sophina yelled at Mariah.

Mariah gave Sophina a look that would make the devil feel uncomfortable. "It. Is. My. Business."

"Now, everyone just hush," Josiah fussed, putting his hands up in the air. Things were about to get out of control and he wanted to maintain order.

"Semira, that was low. I thought you were a better woman, and to bring Natano back here too? You are just mad he wanted me and not you. Get over it!" Sophina shouted, ignoring Josiah.

"You shut up, Sophina," Seth snapped, allowing his anger to overflow. "You are a sick, twisted person. You might have Momma fooled but not me and not Se. You are never welcome in my home or around my children or my niece," he barked and walked out, slamming the door.

"Wait one minute, what's going on? This is my home, and after I got Samson out of here I promised no more violent outbursts. You and Seth can't come into my home and attack your sister. She needs us to help, not condemn her," Ella fussed. "Why did you feel you had to adopt Nalani and not tell anybody?" Ella asked, putting her arms up in the air to calm the tension that was spreading like wildfire.

Again, Ella missed the whole thing. This feud between Sophina and Semira had nothing to do with Natano, and everything to do with Sophina. She was just evil. "I told my brother, Pop, Mariah and all my friends. I just didn't tell you because I knew you'd react like this. You act like Sophina is all you have. She isn't an only child. There are two more of us that act right. All she does is break your heart and ruin this family. I adopted Nalani so she wouldn't have to suffer. Sophina knows why I adopted her," Semira said preparing to leave, but as she was getting up Seth came back inside the house.

"Pop and Momma, I love you, and I'm sorry for raising my voice in your home. I can't come to this house while Sophina is still under the influence. I'm taking my family home, including Nalani. They don't need to hear this," he said and with that, hugged their parents.

"No, Seth, don't leave. I want to know what's going on," Ella implored, looking bewildered and confused. Her family hadn't been in disarray like this since Samson Richards. She needed to know what was happening.

There was rage eating away at Semira's heart. Ella was so blinded that she believed Sophina could do no wrong. "Nothing, Momma. You'd just trivialize it and blame me," Semira told her, gathering her belongings to leave as well.

"Tell her. She needs to know," Josiah insisted.

"What's going on, Josiah?" Ella asked her husband.

Semira swallowed hard and took a deep breath. It was not easy to retell it. She feared how her momma would react. "I adopted Nalani because after Sophina gave birth to her, she was still doing drugs. One night after I placed Nalani down, a man entered my bedroom. A drug dealer named Colt. She sold me to him for the night. He raped me. He stole my innocence that night, and he gave her extra because I was a virgin. Now you know why I avoided relationships, why I stay to myself, and why I can only handle Sophina in small doses. Go ahead, Momma, and tell me how it's my fault. Tell me what I did wrong like you always do," she prompted.

Ella was hushed. Her eyes filled with tears. "Sophina, how could you do that to your sister?" she asked. How could Sophina allow such a horrible thing to happen to her baby sister? Ella felt her heart sink because that meant all these years, Semira had suffered in silence. No wonder she was so angry with Sophina.

Sophina shook her head. She'd hoped never to have to hear of it again. It was a horrible feeling to be sitting condemned. They were pointing the finger of blame as if she were the devil. It was not her fault. Had she been in her right mind, she would have stopped Colt, but she had been as high as a kite that night. Honestly, so what? That didn't mean she was a bad mother. Men had abused her too, but she was not crying about it and stealing other folks' children. She made her tragedy her paycheck. Bad things happened all the time, so why was Semira supposed to get special treatment?

9. Deonna

"Tell her, Sophina. I'd like to know too. You watched him. You heard me scream and did nothing. I implored you to help me. Even after all these years, you have never apologized. That is why you can never be alone with Nalani because if you sold me for a night, you'd do it to her as well. I have given you everything and you ask for more, but you have never said sorry, or even thanked me for raising your child. You knew how I felt about Natano too, but you didn't care. You wanted him just to say you had him. I love you, sister. Why do you hate me?" Semira asked, getting her keys ready so she could leave. "I'm not going to see you for a while, and Momma, I won't be seeing you either. I need a season away. All I ever wanted, Momma, was for you to hear me, to understand, not to rule my life or point out my flaws. You have made your choice. I'm making mine." With that declaration, Semira turned to leave.

"Semira, baby, don't leave like this," Josiah implored, getting out of his chair.

"I'm fine, Daddy. Being raped didn't stop me, being a teenage mother didn't break me, having my sister betray me didn't halt my success, and having my mother choose my sister hasn't dampened my spirit. This won't either. I'm a survivor. I learned a long time ago not to have expectations. Samson taught me that. No one in this house, in this world, will ever take from me again, nor make me feel bad for loving that little girl. I'm giving her what was denied me. That is love; a safe place, respect, and happiness. I'd die before I allow Sophina within an inch of my daughter. I don't care what you say, Momma. I wasn't wrong, but Sophina was. She has been wrong for a long time and I'm not defending her anymore."

Semira walked out with Mariah holding her hand. Seth and Natano followed. Semira forgot he was even there. All she saw was Sophina and her Momma ganging up on her. She didn't care anymore. The truth will set you free, and free she was. She got into her car followed by Natano and Mariah.

"Sis, you want me to take Nalani?" Seth asked, not believing how things had gone down. Semira had kept it all in and now finally she let it go. She was the bravest person he knew. That took so much courage.

"How about you all come to the cookout too? Some of the members of the football team will be there with their family too," she said.

He smiled and agreed.

"Semira, I'm proud of you. You are far stronger than I ever knew. I love you. I will always have your back no matter what," he said, leaning inside and kissing his sister's cheek.

"I know, brother. I love you too," she replied.

4. Deonna

He smiled, got into his car, and followed her. She saw Ella standing on the porch, but she didn't say anything. Now it was time to heal.

Natano was still in shock. How could Sophina be so high she'd sell her own sister? The sister who should be the mother of his child and who he wanted to hold, to soothe the hurt she was feeling. If only he had stayed instead of transferring and forgetting. He could have saved her from that. He would have beaten Colt senseless and thrown Sophina out, but he let his shame be the excuse for abandoning her.

By the time they arrived at Blaine's house, Semira was much calmer. She felt better, even lighter, after confessing the truth. Now she had to find a way to tell Nalani that Natano was her father. She got out of her car and waited for her brother to park. Mariah walked around and hugged her friend long.

"I'm so sorry. I just wish I could take that memory, that pain away from you," she said earnestly.

"I know, Mariah, but adversity draws us nearer to God. The entire ordeal helped me mature as a Christian. I had no one but God to talk to for seven years. If not for Him and Nalani, I would have killed my sister and myself that night. I thought about it. I hated her for a long time. God forgive me, but I did."

Her face saddened when she looked at Semira. That is why she kept it to herself for so long. It hurt all over again to see pain and sadness in the people that you love.

"We are going to get through this," Mariah promised.

"Listen, no gloom and doom. There are some handsome men in there. So get cute before we go in there." she urged, fixing her up.

Nalani ran up to Semira and hugged her too. "We are going to see Uncle Blaine!" she exclaimed.

Semira smiled. She and Blaine were the best of friends too. Semira looked around for Natano and saw him lingering in the distance. "Natano, come on with us," she offered.

"Yeah, Natano, come on. You can meet my cousin Tobias," Nalani offered, running to get him. She grabbed his hand and pulled him to the group and they all walked together. Nalani knew Blaine's house as well as her own home and took off.

"Lani, speak to Blaine before you go to the game room," Semira told her looking around for him.

"Momma, he is in the game room," she yelled. Semira followed her and there he was.

He got up and greeted them.

4. Deonna

"I'm glad you guys finally showed up. Seth and Marybeth, hey how are you both?" he asked giving Seth and Marybeth a hug.

"We're good," Seth said, holding Marybeth's hand.

"Hey, Mariah, I'm so glad you came," he said, kissing her cheek.

"Come on so I can introduce you all. Well, Semira knows everyone for the most part," he said, ushering them to the outside patio. "Y'all get loose and have some fun. Nalani and Tobias will be fine. Lani knows this place like the back of her hand," he intoned, easing the worried look on Seth's face.

Semira sat down. She was not really in the mood to talk to anyone. She'd rather watch and observe.

"Semira, I, well I'm so very sorry about what happened to you," Natano told her. He had no idea and the ride over to Blaine's house, all he could think about was what he had heard. He wanted to make the hurt go away.

"Thank you, but stuff happens you know," she replied, looking at the view and not him.

"Mira, I know I have not been a great friend, but I know you. I know you are still hurting. You don't have to pretend with me." He reached over to caress her hair. The gesture, though kind, made her jump. He removed his hand and looked at her intensely. He had no right to her, but still he cared so deeply for her. Knowing that she was raising and had adopted Nalani made him love her even more, especially after what she'd suffered.

"I do. I'm not opening my heart to you ever again. I've moved on," she quipped, trying not to sound too cold.

He let out a sigh and turned her chair to face his. "I don't know about this Carmine, but I care about you. I wish my first born came from you and not Sophina, but I'm glad that at least you adopted her."

"It didn't and it never will. I can't have children. The attack was so brutal and so much damage occurred, that I can't. No one knows that, but I can't have kids. My sister stole you, and my ability to have children, and my innocence as well. If I let her back in my life, she will continue to take from me. It's what she does. Of course, I hurt. I have a pain deeper than you can imagine. The fact is you chose Sophina, but I got the best gift when Nalani was born. I don't care anymore. I have a decent man who loves my daughter," she retorted, though she was not sure if Carmine really loved her, or if she really loved him. Things didn't feel the same when he called, if he called. He was always rushing her or calling her at times he knew she would not be awake. She was beginning to wonder if he was creeping, and if so it served her right. She knew better than to fall for a basketball player. If she believed the blogs, she was getting two timed. Besides, she was so over Carmine. She was over all men forever. It was a stupid of her to ever want to be loved. It just didn't work for her.

That didn't ease Natano's pain. He only felt guiltier. "So, is he the one?" he asked.

"I don't know. He is the one for now," she said bluntly.

"Does he know what happened?" he asked.

"He knows everything, except my inability to have children."

Natano could no longer conceal his feelings. He loved Semira and always had. "I want you. I want you and Nalani. I dated a bit back in California and Denver, but no one made me feel like you. Don't you think it's fate that I came back, here found you, and learned that I have a daughter? I'll never make the mistake of choosing the wrong one again. I love you. I always have. I love what you do and who you are. So many times I wanted to call you, but I didn't know what to say. I have over a thousand emails that I wanted to send you, but I was too scared to do it. They are still saved as drafts. I respect that someone else is in your life, but I want to be in it as well. Even more so with Nalani being mine, I want a second chance to be a better man," he implored.

Now he wanted to do right? He should have had this epiphany a few years ago. "I have to talk to Carmine. I have to see how he wants to handle this. I will not deny you access to your daughter, never. I also have someone else my life and I'm not doing to him what you did to me," she replied in a respectful tone.

"How long have you two been together?" he asked. He didn't see Carmine as a threat. The truth be told, he knew Mira well, and he loved her. That was what he learned when he'd left in shame because when he tried to date to forget her, she was always the one, the only one.

"We have been dating a few months," she said.

"Okay. Will you just give me a chance? I mean, to be your friend."

"I guess," she acquiesced.

"Tell me what happened that night, after you were attacked. I mean, how did you find out you could not have children?" he asked.

Why did he care? She wanted to forget that night. She never wanted to ever talk about it again, but he wanted to know. He placed his hands tenderly on top of hers. "Well, after it happened and he was done, he left. I could not stop the bleeding and I got scared. My sister was out of it. I got Nalani, drove myself to the emergency room, and walked up to the registration desk. I whispered I needed help because I had gotten attacked and could not stop bleeding. I told her I felt like

9. Deonna

I was going to pass out. They moved swiftly after that and admitted me right away. I was still holding Nalani, she was crying, but I didn't want her to be separated from me. So they asked could they call my parents and I said no. I couldn't face them after that trauma. I called Thomas Calloway, and he came. I asked him to just watch Nalani for me. He stayed with us the entire night. The doctor told me that the damage was so severe I would probably never have children. I accepted that. It's a sin to have self-pity and I couldn't function if I stayed in that space. I didn't know it was possible for a person to inflict that kind of damage, but I got over it. I was thankful for Mr. Calloway that night. We never again spoke of it, but he made sure I was safe after that. He has been there for me ever since," she confessed, but even Mr. Calloway didn't know the entire story.

Natano could feel tears rising inside. She spoke so calmly about the matter. There was no anger in her eyes, more like sorrow, not for herself but for her sister and attacker. It was beyond his understanding how she refused to feel sorry for herself. To be raped, to be denied the gift of having a child, to be denied justice after being assaulted and worse than anything, to know it happened because her own sister sold her. Even though he was a Christian, that kind of forgiveness was beyond him. Even now, her concern was her family. She held that secret from her mother to protect her sister. A sister who violated and lied all the time. He wondered what lies she'd told Semira about him and her. Soph had just been a good time, a lapse in judgment. Semira was the one. She had always been the one. Any man who could conquer her heart would be loved forever. She was goodness. He wished he'd known that back then. "I'm here for you, Semira. I won't betray your trust again. I'm not going to let your sister or anyone else hurt you again. God knows I'm so sorry for leaving you. I will spend the rest of my life making it up to you. You deserve more, but I will give you the very best of me."

Semira smiled. She knew he meant it. She understood from watching her brother, Blaine, and Mariah that people needed to say those words. It helped them deal with the tragedy. She respected that, but it was a little too late. The damage was done, the violation in the past. God brought her through it. He made the pain easier. Now, after sharing it with her family and friends, she was good. She had a fear that Carmine might not take the fact that she could never have children, but for her it was okay. She always wanted to adopt anyway. The pain she felt was that her sister, her own blood, had made her an enemy when all she had ever tried to do was save her.

Y. Deonna

Chapter 11

Sophina rested her throbbing head on the couch as she recalled her past and the horrible pain she'd caused her only sister—a sister that had taken care of her, held her secrets and protected her. Even after she'd betrayed her countless times, Semira always cleaned up her mess. Yet, every chance she had, she just spat in Semira's face. It was disrespectful and wrong. Sadly, it was her who had been jealous of her sister. Semira was strong, smart, and sincere, everything she would and could never be. Too many years of taking drugs of all kinds, had ruined her and the little piece that survived her maltreatment, Dante had corroded. Now, as she heard her mother weep, it was almost too much. Her entire life was caving in around her. She needed her drugs. Living life without that suppressant was more than her delicate nerves could handle.

"Momma, I have to go. I need to get out of here." The house was stifling and growing smaller with each tear her mother dropped. Sophina lifted her tired, broken body off the floor. The only thing she knew to do was run. It was time to leave North Carolina for a while. She needed distance because things were becoming too real. She couldn't deal with reality. She preferred her altered world. Emotions she had locked up were fighting to get free. The truth was that she lacked the strength to deal with them.

"Sophina, don't go. Let me help you. I can get you into a treatment center. You can get better," Ella pleaded, looking at her. It was her fault for letting Samson stay so long and mistreat the children. She had created the perfect storm to ruin her childrens' lives.

"No, Momma, what I got wrong with me can't no center treat. I'm just a bad seed, Momma. Samson always said I would never amount to anything and he was right. I did horrible things to Semira because I wanted drugs. She was right to adopt Nalani. I can't even take care of me. The family is better off without me. I never saw my sister so upset and tortured. For the first time, I saw her, like I saw her pain. I'd rather be high and drunk. It's the only way I know how to live," she confessed with tears pouring from her eyes.

Touched by her confession, her mother walked toward her, feeling that the assault on Semira was just as much her fault as Sophina's because she had allowed Samson to do so much harm. He broke the family. "Sophina, come pray with me. There isn't anything too horrible that God can't fix," Ella encouraged, pulling her daughter down to get on bended knees. "Come on, we are going to pray the Lord's Prayer. Sophina, you have to confess all your sins to Him and ask for forgiveness. As a mother, I have made my share of mistakes too." That was the truth because she made a difference in how she treated Semira and Sophina, but that was because she never wanted her youngest daughter to emulate her older sister.

"Momma, I can't talk to God. I got to get right first. I got to get clean and get presentable," she argued. If ever there was a blackened heart and empty soul, it was her. She feared to even walk into a church.

"Honey, have you been out of tune with God so long you have forgotten? God wants you as you are. He sent Jesus to save sinners, not saints. God will make you clean, God will make you presentable. There isn't anything we can do because we're all sinners saved by God. You just talk to Him," she explained.

"Momma, I don't know how to pray no more. I don't know anything anymore." The tears were falling heavily now. Sophina was scared to confess her sins to God. Afraid that once He knew her faults and flaws, she would be discarded and forgotten.

"I do. I'll pray for the both of us," Ella promised. She held Sophina and cradled her in her arms. Just like she did when she was a child and loved her long. "Sophina, listen to me. It is going to get darker before the light, but if you're patient and just hold on God will carry you through. You have to get help, baby. You have to stop all this you're doing and get better. It's time to heal, no more acting foolish or mistreating your sister or brother. You can't lie to me and your daddy. If you see Dante or take any drugs or drink, as much as it hurts me, I will put you out. I love you. I love all my children, but Sophina you have to want to be better in order to get better."

"I know, Momma. I know you're right."

She rested her head on her mother's chest and longed for the days of her youth. Drugs had stolen her life. She didn't know how to find her way back. She'd lost her Northern Star a long time ago or maybe it just blew out because she refused to follow it. Her mother prayed long and hard for each of her children, and that the pain that seemed to imprison the house would be lifted and the Spirit of God would just remove the hurt, the anger, the betrayal, and the lies. Sophina wondered if her mother was also praying for herself.

~~~

Nalani and Semira sat patiently in the car waiting for Carmine to exit from the double doors at the airport. Semira's mind had been stretched in so many places, she was unsure if she would be able to pick him up. He heard the sadness in her voice but she didn't reveal to him the pain. To be honest, she was not sure if she could even trust him anymore. It had been two and a half weeks since she talked to her mother and sister after telling them the truth and though she felt better, she also had new fears. *Would this turn her sister against her? Would*

4. Deonna

she try to kidnap or hurt Nalani to hurt her? Would she really get help or was she playing Momma, and her and Dante had something else planned? Her knees ached from praying so long about it. Even though she was upset and hurt, what she really wanted was peace. Even as a Christian she felt that peace was hard to achieve. There was still sickness in her soul. She still felt bitter; bitter to her root about how it all had gone down and even about Carmine and Natano. Keeping it all in was creating new wounds that would need to be healed. She didn't like walking around feeling broken and fragmented. Then her mind went back to Natano. What would she do about him and how was she going to tell Nalani? Everyone was dealing with the fact that Sophina sold her for drugs. She was over it to some extent, okay not really, but it didn't sting as much. For her family, the wound was still fresh. It was like secondary trauma and she hated that they were suffering because she suffered. Right now, her emotions were over the top. She didn't know how to verbally express her feelings, but they were a combination of things and her mind ran unchecked like a herd of cattle.

These emotions and feelings of love or lust had her so perplexed and lost. On the one hand, Natano felt so good to her. His touch was not invasive but welcomed, and his kind words were like manna to her brokenness. His ability to know her and

make her fall into sync with him was unmatched by any other
man. One semester was all it took for her to be hooked on him.
She thought after being assaulted he would never want her; no
man would. She was fine not having love. She had Nalani, and
that was enough. Now with Carmine and Natano both wanting
her, it was a hard place to be in. She didn't even know how to
handle them. Would Carmine still want her when he found out
she could not have children? Was Carmine cheating on her? She
knew how athletes worked. She worked with them. So many
had come on to her even those with a family to lose, and she
knew how fast women could be. There were women like her
sister, willing to sell their souls for money, power, and
materialistic things. They were the jump-offs looking to use
powerful and rich athletes to get ahead. She wasn't that kind.
There would be a matter of time when Carmine would want to
have sex and when he found out that she was not ready, he
would probably cheat on her, or even leave her. For all she
knew, he'd already cheated. She recalled the magazines, the
blogs, and the comments. She just wished she'd never met him.
That way it wouldn't hurt.

"Mommy, Carmine is at the door," Nalani said gleefully.

Semira quickly unlocked the doors, got out, and greeted
him with a hug. He kissed her, but she turned so he only got her
cheek, and then he kissed Nalani telling her he had several

surprises. She loved that. Semira drove back to Carmine's house. She and Nalani followed him inside. Since they had been dating, this was only her second time in his home. She preferred he come to hers. He had a nice bachelor pad, but she was wondering if he had brought many women here. She didn't see anything that stood out like women were spending the night, but she was not sure what she was looking for.

"How are my ladies?" he asked, opening his bag and handing Nalani a beautiful doll that looked like her.

"Thank you, Carmine, I love it!" She began to prance around holding her new gift.

"Thanks. That was really nice of you. We've been good. We've had a little drama, but things are better now," Semira explained as she watched Nalani.

"I know. I talked to your brother. Well, I actually called him and, well it was a heavy conversation," he replied, looking serious.

She was unaware that her brother had talked to him. She didn't even know they were close like that. It was unsettling to her. "It's just family stuff. It will die down, as it always does."

"So, are we going to talk about it? Or are you just going to pretend like things are great?" he asked, unloading his bags. From the conversation he'd had with Seth, he knew there was more than she was telling, a pain deeper than she was admitting to, possibly because she still didn't fully trust him. The last time they had spoken there was a strain in her voice, an unsaid agony that she was trying to hold back.

"We can talk later. Right now, you need to unpack and rest. Can I help with anything?" she asked, trying to calm the anger that she had. She was not ready to confront him with the information she had. Her mind, body, and soul could not handle another battle. She was worn.

He smiled. "You can let me kiss you. I missed you a lot," he flirted, walking over to her and embracing her fit body. "I have some good news. My parents are flying in and I'd like them to meet you and Nalani. I talk so much about you two so they are coming and I can't wait."

There was a sparkle in his eye, a glow she had never seen before. It must be wonderful to have that kind of feeling about your parents, she thought to herself. She loved hers, even Samson, but sometimes she allowed her mind to play a dangerous game. The "what if" game that she always seemed to lose. "That is great. I can't wait to meet them," she said, pulling away from his embrace. Her mind was wondering had the same arms holding her, held another woman or two? Again, another dangerous game she'd lose if she didn't stop herself.

"Are you ladies going to spend the day with me? I'm tired and need to sleep, but I want to hang out with you both.

4. Deonna

You can make yourself at home," he offered, wondering why she seemed to be pulling away from him.

"No, Nalani and I have some things to do. You sleep and when you wake up, call us. I can bring you some supper later."

"Awesome, baby. You're so good to me," he gushed.

"Bye, Carmine and thank you for the gift," Nalani told him, walking over and kissing his cheek.

"You're welcome, sweetheart."

Semira grabbed Nalani by the hand and they walked back to the car. Her mind was wondering about the conversation between her brother and beau. What did one have to say to the other that could not be said to her? She buckled Nalani in and decided to drive to Seth's house. She needed to know what Carmine knew. She didn't like being surprised, and she didn't like being discussed without consent. It was less than a twenty-minute ride, one that Nalani knew well and began to get excited the closer they got. She looked in the rearview mirror and smiled at her. There was innocence in her, an innocence she longed to have again. There was purity in all Nalani said and did. Semira loved that she was always filled with love, joy, and happiness. She hoped she never felt the emotions she had. The anger, the guilt, the shame, and the hate. Sometimes, she felt like a hypocrite teaching Sunday school and harboring anger. It was not right. She had no excuses for her behavior. She made a mental note to do a nighttime quiet time. She needed all the Jesus she could get. That old feeling was rising inside again, and she wanted to defeat it for good, no more Band-Aids. She needed surgery to remove the tumor of hate and anger that was suffocating her heart.

She pulled into Seth's driveway and saw a car unknown to her. She hoped it wasn't company for him because she needed to speak to him. She and Nalani exited the car and she ran ahead of Semira to ring the doorbell. Usually, Tobias would have met them at the door, but not this time. No one came, so she rang the doorbell and knocked. She put her ear to the door to see if she could hear anyone coming. She waited. Finally, her brother came to the door. He looked as though he had gotten the worst news. Her heart stopped beating for a moment. Was it Sophina? Was it her mother? What was wrong?

"Seth, what's going on?"

"Come on inside." he told her, "Nalani, you go on up to Tobias' room. He has a new game he wants to show you." She smiled, hugged Seth and then ran upstairs.

Semira's eyes searched his eyes as she attempted to find out what was not being said. "Seth, tell me what's wrong," she urged.

4. Deonna

"Sis, well, Samson is sitting in the kitchen. Come on, you need to hear this too."

Semira didn't move. She remembered well how mean, cruel, and violent Samson was. She knew that he didn't like her. She was not about to let him verbally attack her. She was still trying to get over Sophina and Momma. She didn't have the strength for Samson, and besides, she came here for something totally different. "No, Seth, I can't do that. I'll go upstairs until he leaves. I need to talk to you, but I can wait until you are done with him," she quipped, turning to go upstairs and hide. Hearing his name brought horrible memories, reminding her of the dark decade of imprisonment she'd had to endure.

"Semira, really, he isn't what he was. Trust me, I won't let him hurt you, and when you see him, you'll understand why he isn't a threat," he calmly intoned, pulling her back off the step and taking her hand. She gripped his hand so hard, she was surprised he didn't make her let go. She followed him, her knees shaking, eyes wide, lips quivering. She drew nearer to her brother. She heard his voice, speaking low and sounding weak. When she walked into the kitchen, she didn't recognize him. He was not the bully he used to be, and his clothing was swallowing him. She watched as he sipped his coffee. She let go of Seth's hand, but she could not go any further. Her feet would not move.

"Samson, this is Semira. You can tell her what you were telling me." Seth encouraged.

He turned around real slow and she almost gasped. He looked like death, his body frail, and his eyes starving and sunken. He couldn't fan away a fly. *Who is this man?* she thought to herself.

"Semira, hey sweetheart, how are you?" he asked smiling.

Semira's face was distorted because she had never ever seen anything so ghastly. This was the man who had tormented her, made her mistrust all men, beat them at will, and had made them watch him beat their mother. This was the man who was partially why she was born. He looked so harmless now, so pitiful and sad. "Hello," she managed to say still not moving.

"I was just telling your brother that I miss y'all. It's been over a decade since I have seen any of you."

"Samson, just tell her." Seth snapped, peering at him.

"Well, I'm sick. My kidneys aren't any good anymore and I need a transplant. They put me on the organ donor list, but I don't know when one will come in. I was hoping that one of you would help me."

Semira was stunned. Then KJV Galatian 6:7 came to mind, *"Be not deceived. God is not mocked: for whatsoever a man soweth, that shall he also reap."* The man who told her she

4. Deonna

was nothing. The man who'd ignored her, who'd loathed her, who'd beat her, had now come to ask her for a kidney. He'd denied her everything and he wanted a kidney. My how the mighty fall. A surge of anger shot through her marrow, followed by negative emotions and the quick thought or revenge and throw every ugly thing he said to her right back at him, but she didn't say anything right away. She took a deep breath. "So you want one of us to give you a kidney?" she surmised.

"Well, I know that your brother can't because of his diabetes, but I was hoping that you might consider. Your brother said that Sophina is really sick as well. I don't want to place any pressure on you."

He had made their lives miserable, left, never apologized and he wanted her kidney. God knows she was the only child who could because Sophina could not stay off illegal drugs long enough to be of help to him. "Samson, I need to read about the procedure first in order to make an informed decision."

"I understand. I do. I just wanted to ask, well, I wanted to apologize to you both for the pain I caused each of you and your mother. Being sick and knocking at deaths door has really given me time to see how rotten and unkind I was to you kids. I'm sorry. Whatever you decide, Semira, is fine with me. I don't want you to feel like my life is in your hands," he said, attempting to get up but being so weak he almost fell over. Seth caught him and placed him back into the seat.

Seeing him look so pathetic and so in need hit her right in the gut. She would never be able to live with herself if he died and she could save him. "Samson, I'll do it," she caved.

Seth jerked his head in her direction. There was no way he was allowing her to make that decision without knowing the risk. "Semira, no, don't say that until you have more information," Seth fussed, looking so shocked one would have thought he had been electrocuted.

"Thank you, Semira. All we have to do is make sure your blood and antigen match. I know it will," he said so thankful his daughter was a better person to him than he had been to her. That was a testament to her mother because his daughter didn't get that trait from him.

Seth shook his head in dismay. Semira always did that, buckled no matter what, but this was a big deal, especially for a man who would not give them anything. If it had been any of them who'd needed a transplant, he would not care. "Semira, can I talk to you in private?" It was time to pull out the big brother card.

She followed him, not sure why he was angry. Wasn't that what he'd wanted her to do? Why else would he let Samson

4. Deonna

tell her he was dying and needed a kidney? "What?" Semira asked.

"Sis, this is Samson Harold Richards, the same man who…well you know what he has done. I don't mind forgiving him, and I don't mind allowing him to stay here. I will even take him to dialysis and doctors' appointments, but I don't think you should be putting yourself out there like that. A kidney, that is serious surgery and you have Nalani to think about now."

"I can't renege on it now. I just have to go through with it. I thought that was what you wanted me to do. He's dying. I can't let him die if I can save him."

"Did you ever think that God might just want him to die? You don't owe him anything. He wouldn't do it for you. Besides, we pray in this family before making decisions. Hello! How are you going to jump in front of God like that?" he fussed.

"I don't know what God wants. He doesn't call me and ask for my opinion. Jesus didn't owe us anything either, but he still died on the cross. He said in Matthew 26:25, "*O My Father, if it is possible, let this cup pass from Me; nevertheless, not as I will, but as You will*". He is our father, and if it is God's will for me to take this cup then I will," she explained, seeking his approval and understanding. He could not do it, and Sophina could not do it. Semira had to do it. She was the responsible, reliable, always do what's right one. She would do it. No matter how bad it was, she would not be the one to take away Samson's hope. Hope was the one thing that no person should be without. Hope had kept her from taking her life as well as taking her sister's life after she sold her to her to Colt for crack. Hope had kept her from getting on a plane flying to California and confronting Natano. Hope kept her prayed up.

"Okay, I don't like it, but you have a point. You know he wants to meet the entire family. He wants everyone here just in case he dies. That means Momma and Sophina and I know you have not spoken to either since the…well the *truth session* we had." His sister was in the wrong profession. The way she could argue made him believe she missed her calling as an attorney. She knew how to shut someone down.

She nodded. "I'm getting over it. Look, I need to know, what did you talk to Carmine about?"

He shook his head. He had forgotten they even had a conversation with all the drama that was now occurring. "He asked me about the assault and wanted to know how you were. He said you didn't sound right on the phone. He asked about Natano, but I told him to talk to you. I did tell him what happened at Momma's house," he confessed.

"Okay. I guess I should get Nalani home," Semira replied.

4. Deonna

"Well, will you come back tonight or tomorrow if I can get the entire family together for Samson? I think he just wants to make peace."

"I can," she said.

He smiled and hugged her long. "Sis, will you take Tobias too. I don't want him overhearing things."

Semira nodded her head. She loved having Tobias as much as he loved having Nalani. "I'll go pack up some clothes and stuff, just in case he needs to stay. If you want, everyone can meet at my house," she offered. She didn't like tension and she didn't like being angry at any of her family. Now that Samson's kidneys were failing, it all felt so trivial. Life was a precious gift and she didn't want to waste any of hers being angry at anyone.

She walked upstairs, got the children together, and they left. She wondered what being a kidney donor entailed. When she pulled up to her house, she was surprised to see Natano already there. This was not what she needed. She got the children out and took each child by the hand. She unlocked the door and told them to go upstairs and play awhile. Then she shut the door and walked over to Natano's car. "Natano, what are you doing here?" she asked.

"I wanted to see you and Nalani. I just thought I would come by and say hello." He wondered if he should have phoned her first. That face she was making made him feel a little uncomfortable.

"You should have called. Carmine is back in town and I have not had the chance to talk to him. There is a lot of drama occurring right now, from you to my mom, to Samson. I just feel like I'm about to explode," she said, looking at him.

"What's going on with Samson?"

"Nothing that needs to be discussed, but can you take a rain check? I need to take care of the children, finish up some work and sleep. I'm really tired."

"Okay, I didn't mean to make your day stressful. It's just that I haven't seen you since the situation occurred at the house." He paused for a moment "I was worried. I just wanted to let you know that I am here for you." He wanted to add that he wasn't running away this time and that he would not give up like he did before. He was a man now, and he was willing to stay and fight for her, for as long as it took for her to see he was sincere.

"Yeah I know, and I appreciate you stopping by," she told him.

"I guess I'll go then," he replied, getting out of the car and hugging her. "You look like you need one."

His arms felt so good around her frightened body, but she quickly removed herself from his embrace. She didn't want

9. Deonna

to become attached to him or even Carmine. She just needed her space from men, from all of them. This was a dangerous place to be in. Now her past and present were clashing and she felt confused. "I have to go."

Something wasn't right. He could feel it when he hugged her. She was breaking, but trying to fake it. Classic Semira, but he wanted to help her. He needed to. "Talk to me, Mira. I know there are a lot of things circling your mind. You are horrible at hiding your emotions. We were really close that year in college. You allowed yourself to be vulnerable with me once. Just let me in so I can help, and not as anything but a friend."

"I'm good," she lied, backing away. She didn't want to have feelings for him, and she didn't want to need him. She could not forget seeing him with Sophina, therefore, trusting him was impossible. She was about to speak again when she heard a car pulling up. She looked around and saw Carmine's SUV pulling up. A fear emerged inside and she didn't know why. It was not like Carmine didn't know he existed. She watched as he parked the car and got out walking slowly as if he were trying to figure out what was going on. Semira looked at him, her facial expression probably telling all of her feelings. "Hey, Carmine, this is Natano," she said, introducing the two.

They shook hands and greeted one another, but both were checking the other out.

"So you are Nalani's birth father?" Carmine asked.

"Yes, but we haven't told her yet. I hope to do so sooner than later," he responded, looking at Semira.

"I wanted to ease her into it, Natano. I can't just say 'hey, this is your dad.' It is a process," she snapped with irritation.

"I'm sorry, Mira. I was just saying."

"I'm sorry too. I didn't mean to sound rude. Please forgive me. It's just today has been complete madness. I can't deal right now, excuse me." She turned and quickly walked inside. This was not how she wanted things to go. She liked having a plan and following it, but she never factored in Samson. He had been out of her life for so long that she pretended he didn't exist and now she was going to give him a kidney. She just needed to sit down and think about things without being interrupted, then she would be able to handle everything.

"Babe, hold up, what's the matter?" Carmine asked, following close behind.

"Not right now, Carmine. I don't want to talk about it. I know I have to, but not right now. I'm going to fix the kids some food and just clear my head," she told him, walking into the kitchen, her hands shaking. She hated to be like this. What she needed was a broom, mop, and some Mr. Clean. She thought better when she was cleaning up.

"Semira stop, just stop for a minute," he demanded.

She felt him come up behind her, his long arms holding hers and he pulled her against him. Then he turned her around. "What is it?"

"It's life. I went to see Seth after dropping you off. I was over there for like two hours. Samson, my biological father, he was over there. He needs a kidney transplant because he'll die without one and I said I'd give him mine. I know it's crazy, but I can't let him die. I haven't spoken to my mother in weeks. So, Seth said that Samson wanted the entire family together, I guess, to ask for forgiveness just in case he doesn't make it. I invited them here to make things right. Then I pulled up and Natano is here and it is just too much. So many things have occurred since you have been gone. I'm tired," she expounded, not realizing her body was shaking.

"Babe, just go up to bed and rest. I want you to sleep. I'll order pizza for the kids. Let me help you, I mean it. I don't mind." He held her until she stopped shaking.

She nodded in agreement. Semira went upstairs and he followed. She stopped at Nalani's room and she heard sweet little voices laughing. She opened the door and asked if they wanted pizza. She sent them downstairs with Carmine and she rested her weary head. As soon as her eyes closed, all the things on her mind became a movie. She was watching her life and she could not control it. Instead, she was being controlled by it. It seemed to always be like that. Her reacting to the problems in her life but being defeated. It was hard trying to be the good passive one when she was burning on the inside. Constantly, she swallowed her pain and now it was eating her. It never paid to keep secrets. They only festered.

"Carmine, where is my sister?" Seth questioned as he walked inside. He searched the den and was shocked to see Natano playing with Tobias and Nalani. He looked back at Carmine, but no explanation was given.

"Your sister's in bed. Me and the kids, and Nat over there have been eating pizza and watching kiddy movies," he explained, smiling.

"Is Semira okay?" he asked, concerned.

"I think once she has rested she will be. She said something about Samson, kidney transplant, and a family meeting," he summarized, recalling how she'd spoken a mile a minute.

"Yeah, that sounds about right. I came to check on her because, well, she was not answering her cell phone. I'm going to wake her up. I need to talk to her."

4. Deonna

"Hey, Daddy, can I stay the night?" Tobias asked, running up to his dad.

"I think that can be arranged. You go back and play with your cousin. I'm going to check on Auntie Se Se."

"Okay, Daddy, I love you," Tobias said and took off running back to Nalani.

Seth walked up the stairs, knocked on Semira's door and walked in.

~~~

Sitting in the doctor's office made Semira feel so uncomfortable, because she didn't like doctor's offices or hospitals. This was not about her. It was about Samson Richards. After this, they were all going to her house to talk, or she guessed Samson would talk. Seth had allowed him to stay at his house. It was a good thing since his wife was a doctor, even though she was a psychiatrist. Semira didn't know much about medical school, but she was sure she had to rotate in all medical disciplines. Semira was also nervous because this would be the first time she saw her momma since the blow-up, and the first time she would have Sophina in her home. She hoped things would go well. She was in no mood to argue or hear lies. She just wanted Samson to say his peace and everyone leave.

She sat nervously, not sure what to expect. After reading about kidney transplants and being donors, she was scared. It

230

was a long process, lasting anywhere from three to six months to make sure the living donor was physically and emotionally prepared to handle the transplant. She would have rather been a nonliving donor. It sounded and looked painful, but it was what needed to be done. She hoped if she needed a kidney someone would offer her one. She did have two; maybe God made people that way to share, and she could function. At least the blood was taken to see if she were a match. She wasn't really worried about it, and figured the doctor called them in to explain how to proceed from here.

Semira looked over to Samson and offered him a smile. It seemed that life was coming back into him. The man had been on dialysis for a while now and she knew he looked forward to no longer having to do that, but there was still a chance that his body would reject her kidney. As angry as she was with him, about how he'd treated her in the past, he was still her father and she didn't wish death upon him. Something about knowing that this man who she'd once feared now needed her, helped her view him differently. She couldn't hate him now or even feel bitterness. She felt sorrow. Hopefully with him getting a second chance at life, he would be a better man. She was optimistic.

The doctor came back into his office, but the look on his face was one of disappointment. Neither Seth nor Samson

4. Deonna

seemed to pick up on it, but Semira did. "Sir, is something the matter?" Semira queried.

He looked up for the folder then at her. A perplexed look came upon his face. "Samson, you said that Semira is your biological daughter, correct?" he questioned.

A perplexed look took over Samson's face at the question the doctor asked. "Yes, why is something wrong?" Samson queried. He'd be praying that his daughter was a match. If the doctor told him she wasn't, well it would crush him.

He was quiet for a moment as if he was trying to decide how to say what he wanted to say. "I'm sorry to tell you this, but Semira's not compatible," he replied.

"What?" they all asked in unison.

He shook his head. "As a matter of fact, she isn't your biological daughter. She can't be according to the blood results," he informed.

to be continued...